GUMBEAUX

Kimberly Vargas

DEDICATION

This book is dedicated to Michael
For the person that he is,
For his ability to inspire others and
For loving me just as I am.

ACKNOWLEDGMENTS

There are too many to list, but you know who you are.
Thank you for touching my life.

CONTENTS

January 5, 2010

J.P. Deacon
Orion Publishing
One Market Place
Bethesda, Maryland

Dear Mr. Deacon:

I wanted to express my deepest appreciation that you have agreed to write my biography. Your reputation as a journalist of factual integrity was one of several reasons I approached you for this assignment. There have been many inaccuracies printed about the Fait family over the years, and this is an opportunity to set the records straight.

After much deliberation/consideration, I have decided to disclose my diaries for your perusal. They span the years of 1986 to present day. Through them you will gain greater insight into the Fait "art empire", as you described it during our last conversation.

Thank you and please know if you have any questions. I look forward to your response.

Regards,

Mary Fait
Musée Fait
100 NW Embassy Avenue
Washington, D.C.

1 DEAR DIARY

January 1986

I've never kept a diary before. Scary stuff. Let's see how it goes. My name is Mary Veronica Fait and I'm sixteen years old. I lost my parents about five years ago. They died on the way back from Chesapeake Bay. They were driving home with my Uncle Claude. One minute they were all excited about coming home, the next Claude was calling Grandma Marguerite in a panic, crying because he lost control of the wheel and drove the car off an embankment. My parents both died and Claude survived. I survived too, but am not quite the same.

Claude (Dad's brother) is now my guardian. Grandma Marguerite is in a nursing home and there is no other option. Claude used to do a decent job of taking care of me but started drinking a couple of years ago. Things have gotten progressively worse. He gets very mean when he drinks. When he's sober, everything is fine. Lately, he's not sober much. Losing my parents has been purgatory every day on earth. It's been hideous and frustrating and lonely and angry and mad and sad and miserable and sometimes I just want to walk off a tall building.

We're not a normal family for many reasons, but primarily because my grandfather was Jean-Luc Fait. In case you're not an art person, Jean Luc-Fait was one of the most successful artists of the 20th century. He was a Modernist, a contemporary of Picasso and a he-man in general. Granddad lived from 1890 to 1979. He died when I was ten. He came to America in 1921 and set up residence in New Orleans. About thirty years later, he and Grandma Marguerite moved to Washington, D.C. They bought our present home, a huge place on Capitol Hill.

Things were just starting to normalize after the death of my parents when Claude decided to turn our family home into what it is today, the Musée Fait. He brought back Granddad's paintings from their worldwide tours and traveling exhibitions and had them displayed at home. Then, with the assistance of our family lawyer, Dante, Claude followed the appropriate steps to turn our Victorian on Capitol Hill into a museum.

People are more than happy to pay a mint to visit the home of one of America's greatest painters. We had always been comfortable, but with Claude running things, the money really started rolling in like you wouldn't believe. Celebrities rent our house during off hours and use it as a bed and breakfast. Our backyard has become a hot spot wedding location. Granddad would have hated it. He was a private man who wouldn't have wanted strangers running around his house, touching his things.

Grandma Marguerite thinks all of this is a great way to celebrate Granddad. She told me to play ball, so I play ball. Claude uses me as his companion to accompany him to fundraising events. I know when to laugh at his stupid ass jokes, when to smile at guests and when to excuse myself so the adults can discuss adult business. Claude and I really know how to work a room. He says I'm his lucky charm, his ace in the hole. He says that as long as I'm around, nothing is impossible for him. That was very flattering for a while. Now it just makes me sick.

Claude took some wine courses to become a sommelier a while back. Just to let everyone know how cultured he is, probably. There is no telling which bottle it was, but he crawled inside one and has yet to come out. Ever since he became a certified wino, his behavior has become increasingly disturbing. I confronted him about being such a cheesy snob (he insisted on a Ralph Lauren Christmas one year, in which all our decor had to be only from that designer). Claude didn't appreciate my honesty and we started not getting along so hot. Then, when he started drinking not just wine but all things alcohol, things went from bad to worse.

Grandma Marguerite used to keep Claude at bay, but now he just walks all over her. Dante told me that Grandma is getting rather old and doesn't have the same kind of joie de vivre that she used to have. I know Dante well enough to understand that he's gently implying that senility is setting in. So you see, I have absolutely nowhere else to go.

There's a good person deep inside of Claude, but he's very sad, as I'm very sad. We are both very sad. We're mourning the situation in our own ways. I "love" Claude or whatever, but I don't like him when he drinks. He drinks all the time, so there you go. There's no one to talk to, and I'm scared to be writing all this stuff down but will explode without some kind of release. All the people who work for us act totally weird now. They're scared of Claude. He's paying their salaries so they walk on eggshells all the time.

Only my tutor, Dr. Jonas, knows what's going on. He noticed a cut on my wrist and knew it wasn't really an accident. He said that life can be amazing, so there's no reason to check out early. He said to study hard and to get good grades on the entrance exams for college. He said college would launch me to liberty. Then he got a small book out of his briefcase and handed it to me. It was Ralph Waldo Emerson's "Self-Reliance." He said it would give some illumination to these dark days.

The writing certainly made an impression. It made me realize that you have to look to yourself and no one else to find peace. We came into this world alone, and we will go out alone. You can't put your faith in anyone. You're a lone sailor on the ocean. Your decisions symbolize the course you charter. Your thoughts steer the movements of your boat through life. Are you going to pave the way yourself or listen to others? If the people who you listen to are wrong, you'll hate them for steering you badly. If you are internally guided, you will have made your own decisions and will have no one else to blame. So, pick your poison and live with the consequences.

January 1987

I haven't written for a long time.

Tonight a visitor to the museum set fire to our velvet curtains. He was obviously nuts and security removed him. Living here totally sucks now. We have no privacy and live in a freaking fish bowl. It's all Claude's fault.

I want to kill Claude, but don't know how to get away with it. Once in a while, things get so bad that I don't care if I do get caught and make a move. God must love that guy, though, because nothing I've done has worked. Not even close. I've strategically placed marbles at the top of the stairs. I've poured a gallon of ammonia and bleach in the toilet while he was taking a shower. I've filled the garage full of carbon monoxide and left him in there while he was passed out drunk in the car. Poisoning him is risky, but it might work, if I could ever get my hands on some arsenic. Each time I try and fail, there is a sense of relief, and then there is the shame of being such a coward.

January 1988

Sometimes the only thing that gets me through life is my cat Matisse. He's a fat Siamese cat with blue eyes. He follows me everywhere like my shadow and sleeps on my head at night. His purring is very soothing and helps to relax my nerves. Matisse and I hang out in my room, listening to music for hours.

I made the regrettable comment to Claude that it would be nice if people didn't have to feel their hearts pounding in their chests all the time. Apparently not everyone feels that way. Five minutes later he forced me into the car and was driving to the nearest hospital like a drunken madman. **They couldn't find anything wrong with me. He yelled at the nurses in the emergency room and told them they were overpaid hacks. It was so humiliating. I tried to discreetly apologize to them, but Claude overheard me. That made him even angrier so he dragged me back to the car by my ponytail.**

On the drive back home, Claude was still pretty loaded. He was trying to hold it together for my sake but he's a lousy actor. I told him to try not to lose control of the wheel and he knocked the wind out of me. My face still hurts. Someday it will be time to go off to college. We both just have to survive until then.

January 1988

A new year, a new hope.

Claude doesn't want me too far out of his sight, since I'm pretty much his indentured servant. He pulled me out of high school to have me home schooled. I'm seeing more and more of Dr. Jonas, since he's no longer just my tutor but basically my teacher of everything. He's one of the only people I know. Sometimes I catch myself thinking that Dr. Jonas is cute. I don't know what kind of cologne he wears, but it's intoxicating. I catch myself daydreaming about what it would be like to kiss him, and then feel bad about it because he's a happily married man. Besides that, he's got to be like thirty years old or something and I'm a biscuit away from being jailbait.

Today I was sitting in the library, filling out college applications. Claude gently took them away and placed them on top of the crackling fire before us. He smiled like a deranged game show host and said, "You're going to Georgetown. I've placed some calls, and they're expecting you for the 1989 fall semester."

When I told him I wanted to go away to school, he just shook his head. "I need you here, Mary. You can't go away for school. You need to stay here with me to help run the Musée Fait. You're going to be in charge of this one day. Your destiny is to carry on the family legacy, same as mine. You'll go on to educate the whole world about my father and your grandfather. We have to carry on his legacy— that's why we're here."

Maybe it is and maybe it isn't. Claude has cheapened everything Granddad was about. He's turned the great Jean-Luc Fait into a caricature, a cartoon. The Smithsonian and most of the Washington D.C. museums are free, and charge no admission to the public. But that's not how it's done at our museum, son. Not at the Musée Fait. Dante says that Claude is making serious bank.

Nothing has been able to get me through the last few years except for fantasizing about escape. The most reasonable and socially acceptable means of vanishing appears to be via attending college out of state. Claude is drinking more heavily than ever. He gets hooked on one kind of liquor, stays with it for several weeks, and then switches to something else. Knob Creek is flavor of the month. Each time Claude gets sauced, I make sure to take something valuable from him. He buys a lot of fine art, but doesn't keep very good track of his purchases. It's fairly easy to rob his dumb ass. Claude's drinking keeps him from being observant. He's an easy target that way. Remind me never to drink. Drinking makes you unreasonable, belligerent, and stupid. Not a good combination.

I liberated (some may say "stole"; I prefer "liberated") a very nice vase from him last year. Ming Dynasty, it turned out. Long story short, The Girls and Boys Club got a huge check from Sotheby's. One of their representatives came over with a van full of children, and they all thanked Claude for his generosity. Claude knew it was my doing but took credit for the whole thing so he wouldn't look ridiculous. It's our little game, fun for me and not for him. Until he sobers up, he doesn't deserve to have nice things.

Since my parents died, all the things I loved about D.C. have become bittersweet and full of sadness. The Smithsonian, Eastern Market, Embassy Row, Foggy Bottom, DuPont Circle, Tyson's Corner, the Watergate Hotel, the Kennedy Center. None of these things are fun to see or think about anymore. Not even the memorials can bring me any peace these days.

I used to spend quite a bit of time at the Lincoln Memorial. It's nice to be in the presence of a man I can respect. I used to sit next to Abe and look up at him and think that it would be quite a thing to know him. His statue is almost twenty feet tall, and he's seated. The columns at the memorial are so wide you can't even begin to wrap your arms around them. Then of course, there are all those lovely words from his speeches, engraved in stone. The permanence of that is very calming to me. I have always loved standing at the top of the steps and looking out over Washington. All that white marble, so clean and polished. It seems like nothing bad could ever happen at the Lincoln Memorial (especially at night, when it is lit up and glowing), but even that hasn't been a good fortress of solitude lately. I just want out, and to be anywhere but here.

February 1989

I've been applying for college under an alias: Veronica Fey. Veronica is my middle name, and I just changed the spelling from Fait to Fey. This alias has enabled me to apply for colleges without being asked if I'm related to the Fait family. No one gives scholarships to people with Picassos hanging in their living rooms.

One school looks very promising—Audubon College. I'm interested in the school for several reasons. First, they have a recognized art program that's very impressive. I could learn to be a great painter, like my grandfather. Second, it's right outside of New Orleans, Louisiana. Granddad was French and loved New Orleans. Third, New Orleans is over a thousand miles away from Washington D.C. Fourth, it's very reasonably priced for a private school. If I could take out some student loans or earn a scholarship, I wouldn't have to rely on Claude for anything.

The school wrote back and said they were interested in meeting me. They offered to pay to fly me down there, along with a guest. It's time to tell Claude what I have been up to. He's been in Paris for some convention at the Louvre (I faked a panic attack just to get out of going). He gets home tonight, so we'll have to have a little talk.

March 1989

I will be visiting Audubon College soon with America's Finest Bastard. Why he is pretending to care this week is beyond comprehension. He finally agreed to go visit the school with me. He said he thought the alias was actually a good idea; he doesn't want anyone to kidnap and ransom me.

In return for his gracious appearance at Audubon College, I have to go with him to three society functions over the next month to gain even more support for Musée Fait. This is no way to live. It's time to get away from this pretentious, phony existence and move somewhere visceral and real. Louisiana seems to be those things.

March 1989

We arrived today in Bayou Bend, Louisiana. Bayou Bend is a sleepy little southern town on the edge of New Orleans. Claude disapproves as usual. On our flight to New Orleans, he acted like the worst kind of bitch. "We have our own jet, why are we flying coach with all the losers?" He doesn't get it. You can't fly under the radar in a jet. A kid behind him kept kicking his chair, making him nuts. It was awesome. Claude ordered six travel-sized bottles of Bailey's and drank them one after another, right out of the bottle. No ice or anything.

Our driver took us through New Orleans and into the French Quarter. We turned a corner and the strains of jazz playing became more and more audible. It seemed as though Europe and the Caribbean had been blended together to create a new world. We walked around for a while, looking at Jackson Square. Claude did appreciate being able to walk around the French Quarter with a drink in his hand the whole time. After a cursory look at old New Orleans, we left for Bayou Bend, which was about a twenty-minute drive from the French Quarter.

Bayou Bend is the essence of southern hospitality. The town is darling. Most of the buildings and houses are at least fifty years old. The people here really know how to make a person feel welcome. Upon arrival, the hotel staff served us the most fantastic iced tea you've ever had in your life. It came garnished with succulent orange slices and fresh mint. They were presented to us in silver goblets, which were super icy cold. I'm going to have another one in a minute because it's pretty warm outside. But before teatime, I want to tell you about the man I met today. He knocked me out. He really, really did.

His name is Dr. Richard Landry. He's the head honcho of the art department. I was sitting in the lounge with Claude, waiting to go on a tour. Dr. Landry came out of his office and was pretty cute for an old dude. He had dirty blond hair and emerald green eyes with gold flecks in them. He should get his eye color patented, like UPS brown or Barbie pink. He was very nice, showing us around, looking at my sketches, asking about my favorite art media. He knew what he was talking about. It was cool hearing him talk about the great painters who had influenced his life. The more he talked, the more interested I became. Yes, he was very attractive for an old dude. Uncle C seemed to zero in on my brainwaves and started hurrying us out of there. When I shook Dr. Landry's hand good-bye, my whole arm went to Jell-O and warmth surged through my body.

"I don't think it's appropriate to have teachers that look like *that*," sneered Claude. What a reaction. Dr. Landry was completely professional and polite the entire time. It's not as if he was dancing around in a thong or something. And then—get this—Claude said, "If we were married, you wouldn't act like that. You can't act like that around your future husband. Just so you know."

"I really don't understand the connection," I yelled. "Why are you referring to married people and to us in the same sentence? Don't get *confused*, Claude. I'm your niece, your brother's *child*. What is the matter with you?" Claude knew he was wrong and crawled further into his bottle, pulling the cork in behind him.

Claude doesn't want me to go away for school. He views Louisiana as a cultural wasteland and a total joke. He's pissed off at Audubon College for trying to help me. I don't think he'll be donating a building anytime soon. They'd be lucky to get a shrub out of him. He's even offended by the attractiveness of the staff—but my mind is made up. It's time to light out for the territory.

April 1989

Today Claude got so drunk that he threw me against a bookcase and kissed me on the mouth. I begged him to leave me alone, but his hand started going up my shirt so I brought my knee into his groin. Then he grabbed a candlestick and hit me with it a couple of times. I threw a heavy ashtray at his head and almost got him, but he ducked. I ran out of the library and locked myself in the bathroom. He banged on the door for what seemed like hours as I cried my eyes out, hugging the bath mat as if it was a teddy bear. Eventually he wore himself out and went away.

After brushing my teeth five times with peroxide and baking soda to get rid of his nastiness, I went hunting for black widow spiders outside by the recycle cans and eventually found one. It cast a fearsome shadow. The red hourglass on its abdomen was absolutely beautiful, a work of art. It was a pretty big spider. Two or three would have been better, but you have to work with what you've got. I scooped it into a jar and brought it inside. Claude was passed out drunk in the library, across several nudie magazines. I dropped the spider on the cuff of Claude's bathrobe, near his wrist. It was almost too easy.

As if by divine intervention, my eyes landed on a picture of my parents on his bedside table. There is no way they would want me to kill Claude. I corralled the spider back into its jar and returned it to the recycle bins. I was so frustrated and angry with myself—went to bed and cried for hours. What a coward. I don't have the guts to rid the world of him. He is responsible for my parents dying. It should have been him. It really should have been him.

May 1989

For a while there, it didn't look like escape would be possible. Claude has been so against my decision to go to Louisiana that he refused to pay the tuition. That dirty bastard isn't holding me hostage. My parents would have never allowed this to happen if they were here. He needs to die. There's got to be at least one hungry thug out there with nothing to do.

In desperation, I wrote Dr. Landry a letter. To paraphrase, it said, "Thanks for showing us around, but my Uncle won't pay for me to go to college unless it's within a ten-mile radius of our house. This is because he is a complete tool." Then I pulled out the big guns—the death of my parents. As shameful as it was, my letter disclosed that my parents were deceased and that my guardian was an alcoholic. Using that to get a scholarship was pretty low. It was completely out of line to open up like that to a stranger, but playing the sympathy card seemed like my only hope. The end of the letter was way over the top. The last line was something about wanting to "reside amongst the bayous." Pretty pathetic, I'll admit it—but it worked. Who knows what kind of connections or savior complex Dr. Landry has, but Audubon College offered me a scholarship two weeks later. A totally free ride. Fifteen thousand dollars per year! Enough for tuition, room, board, and financial independence.

To maintain the scholarship, all I have to do is take Louisiana History classes and have dinner annually with the couple that foots the bill. They're super old and apparently give a ton of dough to the school. They must like to see the kids their money is shaping, so they don't get buyer's remorse.

I can't believe this is happening; it just seems too good to be true. My tutor was right; it was worth working so hard and getting good grades. Freedom is sitting across the table. Time to grab for the brass ring. There is only one downside to moving. They don't let cats in the dorm, so I won't be able to bring Matisse. But eventually I will probably be able to get an apartment or something, and will bring him to Louisiana with me then.

August 1989

I just told Claude about my scholarship to Audubon College and he went ballistic. No surprise there. I didn't mention it until the dorms were open, so I'd have a place to go. Claude said he was cutting me off without a cent. He's probably been having fantasies about doing that for years now, ever since my parents died. He said to forget about any financial support whatsoever and that defying his authority + moving away = no $$$. He said I was a spoiled princess and was in for a real shock once I left the castle walls. He said that I was choosing what kind of people I wanted to be around for the rest of my life.

In response, I calmly cut up my credit cards as Claude watched. He's quite the voyeur. Then I tossed the pieces over our heads like confetti. He grabbed a fifth of amaretto liqueur and started to drink it straight from the bottle. As he ranted and raved, his overly sticky sweet breath hung in the air.

"I don't want any part of you or the Musée Fait," I finally said to shut him up. "I'm starting a new life under a new name. You can have the money and the art. You can have all of it and all of this. I don't want it if you're part of the total package."

He was dumbfounded. Apparently he hadn't received the memo RE: You can't always get what you want. "You can't do that, Mary. You can't do that. This is so selfish of you. It's so unlike you."

"That's right. It's time for me to be selfish. I'm tired of being your ventriloquist's dummy all the time. I'm going to go and live for myself. Not for you, not for Musée Fait—for myself. And if you don't like it, I suggest you punt."

"You are a stupid girl, Mary."

"No. You're just jealous. You were jealous of Granddad because he was a star. You were jealous of my parents because they had each other. You're jealous of me because you think you need me, and you actually resent me for it."

"Why would you say something like that?" he slurred, face screwed up into fake devotion.

I laughed with disgust. "Because you told me so, Claude. You have no recollection of it, though, because you're a raging alcoholic."

"You shouldn't say such things, Mary. You may regret them later on." He was pretty groggy, but his anger was waking him up a little.

I put my face about two inches in front of his, to make sure the next message was crystal clear. "I only have one regret in life, Claude. It's that they died and you didn't. It should have been you. It really should have been you."

Oscar Wilde once said that if you're going to tell people the truth, make them laugh. Otherwise, they'll kill you. Perhaps I had expressed a little too much honesty, because Claude struck me in the face with excessive force. He used the heel of his hand, as if spiking a volley ball. He sent me flying into a table. My tooth didn't go all the way through my lip, but enough to produce a significant amount of blood on the Oriental rug. I recalled that the rug had once belonged to Elizabeth Taylor, and then passed out. When I woke up and was able to turn my head enough to look up, he was gone.

I'm going outside now to go see if there are any more black widows out by the trash bins.

2 AUDUBON COLLEGE

August 1989

One magical summer night—a night that will live in infamy or what have you—I packed up all my things and got out of Washington. You have to drive across like ten states to get from D.C. to Louisiana. It took forever but it didn't seem like it. It felt as though I had located the secret passage of the Underground Railroad and was hauling ass towards freedom. Driving across the Louisiana state line was so liberating. A huge sign greeted each driver warmly: *Welcome to Louisiana.* It looked like a code of arms, a family crest. Cobalt blue with a pelican on it. An intoxicating and cathartic freedom began settling in. Fresh start! Clean slate!

I read somewhere that the lawless drift as far away from the seat of government as possible, throughout history and across all cultures. New Orleans is ridiculously far away from D.C. I envision Louisiana as a somewhat defiant state where people do what they want. A place for people who want to enjoy life and have a good time and to have life experiences and adventures. Where do you go when you disappear? The answer is different for everyone. I chose Louisiana.

Upon reaching Baton Rouge, I sold my car at the first opportunity. Right off the highway was a dumpy little second-chance style car lot. Most college students don't drive Bentleys. Fitting in was the name of the game, so it had to go. I bought a Volkswagen Rabbit convertible, white exterior and interior. The ultimate sorority chick mobile. The car salesman raised his eyebrows a little, but not nearly as much as one might have back in D.C. He seemed eager to assist me in my mission, whatever it was, and he didn't ask any questions that weren't required for the actual sale. I was going to like Louisiana just fine.

Dante insisted I come by to see him before leaving town. Dante is not just our family lawyer, but also head of legal counsel for

Musée Fait. He helped me forge some stuff so I could get away with the alias and escape Claude. Dante tries to be professional, but you can tell he hates Claude and enjoys thwarting him. It's nice to have an ally.

Dante told me that Louisiana is like a whole other country and gave me a synopsis of what to expect in the Deep South. This next part is unreal—he gave me a gun! Does he think I'll be trapping furs with Cajun Pete or something? The only person I need protection from is Claude. Dante said going to Louisiana is like going to a parallel universe and one might as well go armed. He said everyone else would be.

Then he handed me this tiny little gun which looked like a toy. He said, "Just a Derringer, see? No big deal. That's a good gun for women. Very easy to handle." Dante insisted that Dad would be upset if he didn't do what he could to protect me. I tried to tell him I was just going to college and not appearing in a James Bond film, but he wouldn't listen. "The gun is rather valuable, so make sure it doesn't get into the wrong hands." He wouldn't reveal the prior owner's identity. Our family is nuts. You can't throw anything away for fear it once belonged to Napoleon or something.

I am now in charge of what I can eat and drink, my own schedule and time, and with whom I can interact. Not having to get approval for every little thing has been exhilarating. This should be a good place to heal. No one knows me or my life situation. I've had a lot of time to think about who I want to be in my new life, and in my new identity of Veronica Fey. Veronica Fey is an art student at Audubon College. Veronica is fabulous, men dig her, and she's an awesome artist. She is way cooler and more interesting than me. She's going to live the life Mary Fait couldn't possibly live. Mary Fait lives under a microscope and does as she's told. Veronica lives for herself and nobody else. She's smart, self-reliant, and a survivor. She is the best version of me that I can aspire to be.

October 1989

I am loving it here at Audubon College!

Louisiana has really folded me into the warmth of her embrace. Everyone has been warm and welcoming. I've already met a ton of people and been to a million places. The weather has cooled into Indian summer, and leaves are turning a little—not that much.

There are oak trees everywhere; they look mystical and ancient. Spanish moss descends gently from the branches, giving them a deliciously haunted quality. So many people have decorated for Halloween; the intensity around the holiday is surprising.

Earlier tonight I turned in a paper to Dr. Landry. It was about Georges Seurat—easy as pie. I was excited to turn in my paper because of how well it turned out. I left our dormitory and walked across campus towards the art building. The art building looks like a huge plantation house. It has huge white columns and about a zillion rocking chairs across its huge, sprawling front porch. All you need is a few hound dogs and Southern belles and you're back in the Old South.

When I went inside the building, it was pretty much empty. Only the cleaning people were still there. I took the stairs instead of the elevator. The odor of fresh paint permeated the air. The fumes were dizzying—in a good way. I felt a little light-headed walking up the stairs to Dr. Landry's office on the second floor. His door was open and there was a light on inside, but he wasn't around. I put my paper on his desk. Then I arranged it a little differently, then centered it a little better, then turned around—and there he was.

"Why hello, Veronica, I didn't mean to scare you." One of Dr. Landry's best qualities is that he's literally one of the most personable and friendly people you could ever hope to meet. People love him. Why? Because he has a secret power, same as Batman or Captain America or what have you. I figured it out one day in class. Dr. Landry makes every person around him feel special. He's a completely present person. He's so attentive. He hangs on your every word and makes you feel important. He even does it with the payroll clerk who's so old she keeps forgetting to close the vault every time she has to make change for students. People are drawn to him because he makes them feel good about themselves.

"I didn't mean to scare you. Are you turning in your Seurat paper?" asked Dr. Landry. He's a Seurat fiend. We have one hanging on a bathroom wall at home. Maybe one day I'll give it to him.

"Yeah," I said. "Thought I'd get it in today. Tonight. Since Halloween is tomorrow. Night." Whenever I was around him, I started sounding really stupid.

"And what are you going to be for Halloween?" His voice was ever changing and fluid, like quicksilver. It changed tone and inflection based on who he was addressing, as if to make the other person more comfortable.

"Princess Leia," I grinned.

He laughed. "Oh, with the white dress and boots, right?"

"No, in her slave costume from *Return of the Jedi*." I know what you're thinking. But that's what I'm wearing, and he did ask.

He blinked, and then cleared his throat. "I see. Well, don't wear it to class or anything. Let's keep it professional."

"I wouldn't wear that to class." I giggled at the suggestion (but in all honesty would have if he'd wanted me to).

"Well, Veronica, are you interested in joining the Bayou Bend Art Club?" He sat down behind his desk and put on these very professorial glasses that he wears in class. *Super* cute.

"What's the Bayou Bend Art Club?" I sat down in one of the chairs in front of his desk. His desk had piles of paperwork everywhere. The piles themselves seemed to have some semblance of organizational structure, but he had way too much stuff.

"It's a club here at Audubon College," explained Dr. Landry. "We create venues for the student artists to have their own showings and get some exposure.

"Sure, why not? I'd be into that."

Dr. Landry leaned back in his chair, smiling. He was so comfortable in his own skin, like a lazy panther lounging around. "What else are you into?" he asked.

"Oh, I don't know. I like all the artsy stuff, of course. I like food a lot. I like guys a lot." What was I saying? That sounded terrible.

He raised an eyebrow ever so slightly, and said, "Well, Veronica, I'm sure they like you too. What's not to like? Listen, I just have to finish up a couple of things, and then I'm going out for dinner. There's a place across the street from the college. It's called Gumbeaux. I like to think of it as Bayou Bend's version of Les Deux Magots in Paris, a watering hole for some of the world's greatest artists. Care to join me?" He asked.

I wasn't really dressed to go out to dinner, so I declined the invitation, left his office, and exited the building. The sun had set completely. A convertible drove by, and a song was playing on its radio. It was something to the effect of wishing upon stars and that your dreams would come true as a result.

The October air was full of spices. I was suddenly starving. Dr. Landry's office desk lamp was the only light against a midnight black backdrop. I could actually see Dr. Landry in his office, typing away. On his face was that contended peace you only see in those who love what they do. Happy people who love what they do are as rare as Renoirs. I wanted to know the kind of peace he had, so I lingered another moment, shivering in the cool, quiet darkness.

Walking back to the dorm, I wondered what kind of conversation we would have had at dinner. Not that it really matters, of course. Adoring him from afar is the only option. I know what happens to mortals who get involved with the gods.

November 1989

Made a new friend! His name is George Graves. George has sandy blond hair, green eyes and is on the tennis team. He has lived in the area all his life and looks like he walked out of a GAP advertisement. He's funny and smart and has a ton of energy.

George is in the art program here at Audubon and is with me in a couple of classes. We really connected Halloween night, when I wore my Princess Leia costume. He is into Star Wars too. Dorks unite! He said he had a huge collection of Star Wars memorabilia at his parents' house. The collection has its own room and everything. I begged him to take me there to see it sometime. He suggested I come home with him for Thanksgiving to have dinner with his family. The invitation was music to my ears and I almost hugged him.

Yesterday he introduced me to boiled crawfish. It's not crawfish season, but we went to a place where they farm them and sell them year round. I had never even seen crawfish before, but they pretty much just look like little lobsters. George drove me to a food shack on the side of a country road where they sold them by the pound. A canopy of oak trees stretched overhead. The crawfish was being boiled in an enormous black caldron. The air smelled of cayenne, lemon and bay leaves. Enticing, fragrant steam billowed from the cook's caldron in all directions. I looked into the pot and saw not just crawfish, but new potatoes and sections of corn on the cob.

George told the cook that we wanted to start off with four lbs. of crawfish. The cook was selling the crawfish for $3.00 per lb. George scoffed, said that was "highway robbery" and proceeded to negotiate with him. The cook told George to take it or leave it, so he acquiesced. The cook scooped up a huge pail of crawfish, potatoes and corn and handed it to George. Behind the crawfish shack were several picnic tables. The tables had holes cut in the middle of them, and there were trashcans under the holes in the tables. You just threw the remains in the trashcans as you sat there and ate. It was almost too much. I just stared at all the little lobsters, wide eyed. "Who's going to crack them open for us?" I asked quietly, thinking that might be a stupid question before I even said it.

George started laughing. "Jeeves, my butler." Then he looked around in irritation. "Where is he? Jeeves, if you can hear me, you're fired! Fired, I say!" George sighed. "Oh well, Veronica, too bad. Looks like you're going to have to do a little work here."

I wrinkled my nose. "I'm going to need some latex gloves if you want me to take apart those things."

George sighed to convey his annoyance. "You're going to have to be a little less high maintenance if you want to hang out with me. Now, watch and learn from the master." George pinched the tail of a large crawfish and in one precise, swift motion, was able to extract the crawfish tail from its shell. It was left completely intact.

I awkwardly reached for a crawfish and held it gingerly by one of its legs. "I don't think I can do this."

"Do it. It's worth it," George assured me. I watched as he shelled a few more crawfish, as if he had been doing it all his life. Then I realized that he probably *had* been doing it all his life. I looked around for silverware and saw there was none. The people at the other wooden picnic tables didn't seem to have a problem with it. They were all eating with their hands. No one seemed to care about their hands turning orange from all the cayenne pepper. I didn't want that stuff under my fingernails; I was worried about getting it in my eyes. George was watching me and seemed to be able to read my mind. "Veronica, you told me you came here because you wanted to start a new life. If you don't eat crawfish, and if you don't get excited about all that is Louisiana, I'm afraid we're not going to work out. Although I've optimistically put you in 'friend' status, you're running the risk of being downgraded to the status of 'known associate.'" It sounded like he was kidding, but he wasn't kidding. Not really.

I sighed and cracked open a crawfish. The first one spewed a little liquid down the front of my shirt. I squealed and George almost fell off the picnic bench laughing. I got better at it, though. The crawfish were delicious and so were the potatoes and corn on the cob. We ate the four lbs. of crawfish, and then went back for another three. I had crawfish juice and cayenne pepper all over me. George was immaculate.

When we were done, I started to walk away from the table. George called me back. "Hang on, Queen Elizabeth, you left kind of a mess. Clean it up before we head out."

I looked at the paper towels and a few empty crawfish shells. "Don't they have people to clean that up?" I asked. I didn't mean it in a bad way, but George said I was spoiled. I'm not spoiled, not at all. I just think if you go out to eat, you shouldn't have to clean up.

Does that sound bitchy?

November 1989

Louisiana History class is a trip! The teacher is Dr. Harris. He's very nice and is all about Louisiana. He has this terrific southern accent. On the first day of class, he and his wife showed up with a deep fryer and an espresso machine. They made beignets and café au lait for the students. Beignets are like French doughnuts, sans the hole. They were steaming hot and snowcapped with powdered sugar. The coffee was delicious, decadent, and inviting. It had a sweet, smoky taste and aroma with hints of dark chocolate. The first taste sent a ripple of warmth through my soul.

Dr. Harris asked where we were all from, so we went around the room and stated our names and hometowns. Some of the responses included Missouri, Texas, Arkansas, Oklahoma, Alabama, and Tennessee. He asked the expatriates among us why we had moved to Louisiana. The consensus was that we had all been intrigued by Louisiana. He was happy to hear it and said since we were having coffee and chicory, he'd discuss its origin. Here's what he taught us:

Coffee first came to America by way of New Orleans back in the mid-1700s. The French brought coffee with them from Martinique as they began to settle their colonies along the Mississippi River. The coffee/chicory combo was developed during France's civil war. Since coffee was hard to get during wartime, chicory was used to make it go further and add additional body. Chicory is the root of the endive plant. Endive is a type of lettuce. The root of the plant is roasted and ground. It's added to the dark roasted coffee to soften the bitter edge. Nova Scotia's Acadians brought this idea and other French customs to Louisiana. It's heavily entrenched in New Orleans's culture. Cafe du Monde is a great place to find it; it's been a landmark in the French Quarter since the 1800s. Twenty-four hours a day and seven days a week, you can get a hot cup of coffee and chicory. Coffee and chicory is often served *au lait* which is French for "with milk." Hot milk is fifty percent of the drink.

Dr. Harris said that Louisiana isn't made up of counties, but parishes. He then distributed maps of Louisiana with its sixty-four parishes broken out. He said we needed to memorize all of their names and locations by next month, and everyone groaned. It looked like a jigsaw puzzle of French and Indian names. He said we would be learning about Louisiana's rich past and that New Orleans was often described as the most interesting city in America. He called it a cultural melting pot influenced by France, Spain, Africa and the Caribbean. Each contributed to the culture, and nowhere was this more concentrated than the actual port of New Orleans.

Everyone was pretty enthusiastic about the class, except for one obnoxious boy in the back. He wanted to talk about how New Orleans had already seen her glory days. Everyone turned around to look at him as he catalogued a few high points in her past. It certainly was rude, especially after Dr. Harris and his wife braved the building's fire codes to make us breakfast. Dr. Harris politely shrugged off the comment.

"Cities follow cycles. If you study history, you recognize the patterns. And my friends, Louisiana is getting ready for a renaissance period. Mark my words."

November 1989

We did acrylics on canvas today in painting class. I brought my own acrylics because they're better than the ones provided by the school. Dr. Landry watched me wheel in my roller bag suitcase of paints and begin to unpack a few of them. He seemed surprised by all the different shades of color.

"Veronica, do you plan on always bringing your own paints to class?" Dr. Landry wanted to know.

"If we're painting and using acrylics, then yes. Of course," I told him.

He took a few out of my suitcase and looked at them. I didn't like him touching my things but didn't say anything. "Why do you need two shades of beige this similar? Why don't you just use the ones we have here in class and mix them?"

"First of all, one shade is eggshell and the other shade is ecru. It seems strange that I would have to explain that to you, a man of your position." I watched as he folded his arms in disapproval. "Second, I don't believe in mixing colors."

"What?" He looked amused, like I was five years old.

"I don't mix colors," I repeated, getting a bit sassy with him.

"What do you mean you don't mix colors? Everyone mixes colors," exclaimed the professor. A few other students stopped what they were doing to listen. It was embarrassing.

"Well, I don't, not ever. I think it makes them look muddy. I always use the paint fresh out of the bottles," I tried to explain quietly, not interested in creating a scene.

"That must be why they look so great!" piped in George, who was sitting next to me. "Every time I look at one of your paintings, they just make me feel peaceful." He smiled at me and winked.

Dr. Landry ignored George and his comment. "So you like the colors al fresco, do you? Well, excuse me, Da Vinci, but this is just a class assignment. Is it really necessary to bring in your own paints? It's kind of a distraction. You and your paint-cart-on-wheels here."

"But what if the class exercise turns out well?" I asked, not understanding why Dr. Landry was so insistent about using class paints. "I'm trying to have a consistent style, and I use my signature colors in all my acrylic paintings. I don't want to switch up the colors. It would mess it up. When everything changes and stops being consistent, you just get a big mess."

"You don't get a mess. You get a gumbo. You get a community of colors that wouldn't have existed unless they were able to blend. All the different ingredients in a gumbo are what make it great."

"That sounds messy." I made a face.

"Maybe you're right, it could be considered messy. Life is messy, if that's the way you want to think about it," Dr. Landry pontificated at me. He's a little preachy, if you want to know the truth. He should carry a podium around with him. "But that's a very negative outlook. You're defaulting to a negative perception rather than a positive one. You need to get out of this static universe you've created. You're wired too tight, girl. Loosen up. Try to be a little more flexible. Blend in a few new colors here and there."

Where was this coming from, and just who did he think he could call "girl"? "I don't blend."

"No, you sure don't. In more ways than one." He cocked his head to the side. "You're a bit of a lone wolf, aren't you?"

George had been listening, but turned back to his work when Dr. Landry gave him a dirty look. "I don't know, Dr. Landry," I muttered, hoping he would drop the subject.

"You don't know if you're a loner?" He wasn't dropping it.

"I guess. I just feel invisible sometimes."

"You? Invisible? Hardly. You're part of this class, this school, this art program, and this community."

All of a sudden I had a headache, wanted some air, and excused myself to go outside. Dr. Landry followed me. "I'm not trying to upset you, V," he explained. "I'm trying to show you that your behavior is a little off. It makes you look like a shit head to insist on bringing in your own paints when everyone else in the class is fine with the ones the school provides."

"Did you just call me a shit head?" My jaw dropped so wide that it's still kind of sore.

"Not exactly, but sort of. I said it makes you *look* like a shit head to insist on bringing in your own paints—"

"How dare you!" I cut him off. "You don't get to speak to me like that!" No one ever dared say a negative word to me in my D.C. life, aside from Claude, and he's family. Such as it is.

"Is that right?" Dr. Landry got in my face and he's like six foot five inches tall.

"Yeah," I responded with considerably less confidence.

"What are you going to do about it? Call the Dean of Students? Do you think he would really be surprised to hear that a snippy little freshman was acting like a shit head and needed to be called out on it? You're not the only shit head here or anything, so don't take it so hard."

He patted me on the head. It struck me as a patronizing gesture and I almost smacked him. "You should watch yourself. You can't act like this," I informed him.

He had a pretty cold laugh, for such a nice guy. "The hell I can't. This is my class, and you're here to learn a few things. I suggest that you also learn how to blend in and stop being such a prima donna," he lectured. "People hate prima donnas."

"I am not a prima donna!" I yelled, acting exactly like one.

"I have to bring my own paints," he mimicked me. "I'm just slumming it down here in Louisiana. Everyone is so stupid compared to me." He really had my voice down.

"I am not like that!"

"Then stop acting like that," was his next recommendation.

I roughly brushed a tear away and glared at him, which he seemed to find endearing for some reason.

"Sorry if that hurt your feelings, but you needed to hear it. As your teacher, I have a responsibility to help you grow and develop." His voice had softened and was lower by several decibels.

"What? Why?" I was taken aback and probably sounded rude. "I thought you would just help me decide what areas of study to work on and help me find internships. Stuff like that."

"It can be that. It can be just that. Or I can help you in numerous areas of your life. Behavioral change is the kind of change that really matters, and if you want to be successful, you'll listen. Everyone has to make that choice for themselves. Just like in every other facet of life, we all reap what we sow. **Besides,** everyone's got issues. We're all trying to tame the snakes in our heads."

That analogy resonated, for whatever reason. "Yeah. I definitely have some snakes in my head."

"If you have any snakes in your head, they must be fairly small and benign. Little green garter snakes," he joked. "Right?"

"Uh yeah. Pretty much, Dr. Landry," I hedged.

"What do they seem like to you?" He asked, sounding a bit like a highbrow talk show host.

"If you really want to hear about it, they've seemed like anacondas ever since my parents died." Something about him made me want to confess all my sins and shortcomings. Thanksgiving was nearby, and there were all kinds of bales of hay, cornucopias, decorative seasonal squash, and pilgrim-inspired decorations all around the courtyard. Some were classy, some not so much. But they did remind me to be to be thankful that I was finally safe from Claude, and I decided to be a little more receptive about Dr. Landry's constructive feedback.

"I remember your letter, of course," he recalled, scratching his head. His golden hair caught the late afternoon light perfectly. "It was pretty much why we made sure you got a full ride. And you're a very talented artist, of course," the professor was quick to add.

"Of course," I repeated. My parents are taking care of me even from their graves. "Then you may also remember what I said about my uncle. His name is Claude and he is not a nice man, to say the least. Being around him all the time has really messed me up. I can't seem to connect with people anymore. I came here to start a new life. If I hadn't, I would have eventually killed him."

He laughed at my response. "We all joke about our families," he said, "and that's not so crazy."

Before I could censor myself, the truth came out. "I'm not joking, Dr. Landry. At times I wanted to kill him so badly it was awful. My adrenaline's surging, just thinking about it." What a confession. Lock me up now. The words hung in the air, thick like black smoke.

He looked surprised and said, "You don't mean that, do you?"

I had said too much. "Let's drop it, okay?"

"Are you sure you want to stop talking about this?" he asked. "Because I think I can help you." He looked genuinely concerned, which was nerve racking.

"I'll be fine." I was speaking in faith.

"No, I'm not so sure you will. Your emotional state is fragile. If you can't overcome this suppressed pain, you'll continue on your apparent path of solitude. If you don't redirect, you'll eventually end up alone." He looked so confident in his prognosis that it felt like a curse. His words sent chills up my spine.

"You aren't a psychologist, Dr. Landry. You're not qualified to make statements like that." The statement was more to make myself feel better than to serve as a reproach.

"No. I'm not a psychologist. But I'm an old guy and smarter than you are, so just listen for a minute. You can't avoid everything just because it's unpleasant to deal with. You can't have any kind of relationships that way. Interacting with others is part of life you can't avoid. I just don't want to see you miss out. You're quite a girl; you just don't know it yet. All people have the power to charm the snakes, but only if they believe it." Having said that, he went back to class, and I followed without another word.

After class, I took the paints back to the dorm room and looked at all the bottles. The individual colors didn't want to be blended. They were perfect and self-contained in their own individual tubes.

December 1989

Getting ready to go home for Christmas. Stressed about it. We'll see how it goes; maybe Claude and I can smoke the peace pipe or something. Maybe we can let bygones be bygones.

December 1989

When I got home, the first person I wanted to see was Grandma Marguerite. She was working on a crossword puzzle in her room when I came in. She completes the crossword puzzle from *The Washington Post* every day. They are not for the faint of heart.

When she saw me, she looked a little confused. It was clear she was pretending to remember me, but she didn't. Not really. When she got up from her television watching chair to go to the bathroom, I looked at the puzzle she'd left behind. Her penmanship and answers were disturbing. She had tried to fill in the tiny boxes with a red magic marker, and the paper looked as though it was bleeding to death. When she returned, I hugged her and hugged her until she said she had to go to the bathroom again. Then she asked where I lived and how long I had been a nurse. I left the room and burst into tears on the other side of the door, feeling more alone than ever.

December 1989

What a night. I woke up and realized that Claude was standing over my bed. He was holding a big drink in one hand and a small flashlight in the other. I didn't make a noise or say anything; I just waited to see what he would do. He didn't know I was awake. He just stood there and looked around the room, and then at me in my bed. I pretended to be asleep. I was too scared to move or say anything at all. Playing possum seemed to work. He finally left. I have been shaking ever since.

Everything was fine just a few hours ago. Claude had arranged for some really fancy carolers to sing for Grandma Marguerite and me. They sang to us from the front lawn as powdery snowflakes the size of nickels fell gently from gray skies. He played the piano earlier in the day. Claude is an absolutely fantastic pianist, and we sang Christmas songs and drank eggnog and played Scrabble in front of the fire. He can be charming sometimes, but once you put a few drinks in Claude, all the charm evaporates and you're back to square one. I don't have a psychologist, but if I did, they would probably suggest that I never interact with Claude again. He is so toxic that he can't help himself.

December 1989

This week I was more tempted than ever to kill Claude. He has no idea how lucky he is. I asked him why I couldn't find Matisse, and he said there had been an "incident." Matisse had gotten out, and had been hit by a car. He said he was torn between pretending the cat ran away and the truth. The lie would have been better. He told me this fact in the kitchen as I was slicing tomatoes. He was making comments like it was too bad about my cat, but cats were stupid anyways, and if they were stupid enough to get out, then it was their own fault for getting killed. Sure. He probably got drunk and left the front door open. My hands were shaking because I wanted to put the knife into him so badly. I accidentally cut myself, slicing through the edge of my thumb. Even in his stupor, Claude knew enough to get out of the kitchen. Matisse died under his watch. I should have figured out a way to get him to Louisiana earlier, but I didn't and now my cat is dead.

Later that night, Claude got so drunk that he passed out across his monstrously large desk that probably makes him feel like more of a man. He's the king of the phallic symbol and never even sees it. *The emperor has no clothes* should be tattooed across his forehead. There's a safe in his office, behind a Bernini sculpture. He made the mistake of letting me see the code, so he gets what he gets.

In the back of the safe, carefully wrapped in velvet was a Fabergé egg. I gasped at the sight of it. I had heard that Claude had gotten his hands on a Fabergé egg. He wasn't supposed to have it; it was ill gotten gains. He probably had an Indiana Jones type scouring the globe for more plunder. He was sketchy like that. Mom once said he was "ethically challenged". She and Dad had been talking about how he had bought a Fabergé egg on the black market and they were worried he would get caught and go to jail. They had clammed up the moment they saw me. Only Claude would have a nest egg of Fabergé. I stuck it in my pocket, felt better immediately and decided to head back early to Louisiana.

January 1990

Before I left our nation's capital, I did something pretty bad (aside from liberating Claude's egg, that is). I went to the National Cathedral, went into my favorite chapel and prayed for God to take Claude out permanently. No one else was in there. Good thing, too, since I was sobbing audibly and asking God why He had forsaken me into the care of such a fiend? What was His plan and how much longer did I have to suffer like this?

As soon as I stood up, the stained glass windows darkened, as if clouds had passed overhead while I was on my knees. I can't shake the sinking feeling that He heard me and unleashed something truly insidious. If I could undo my prayers, I would. But vengeance is really God's area anyway. His opinion of Claude is the only one that matters.

When I got back to Louisiana, there had been a recent incident at an offshore oil rig. A lot of birds and fish had become sick from the oil. I forwarded the Fabergé egg to one of my sources so they could sell it for me anonymously. I know it seems hard to wrap your head around, but it's just an egg, after all. The actual value is nothing compared to the perceived value. Anyway, the egg raised over a million dollars, all of which went to Louisiana coastal relief. That will only do so much, but at least it's something.

February 1990

Haven't written in a while. Losing Matisse has really got me in a dark place. All this crazy sadness—can't shake it. Guilt about not spending enough time with him, not ensuring he had the best life possible. Claude probably shot him. He hates cats as much as he hates me. Dr. Landry said the experience brought back all the pain I felt over my parents dying. I still can't believe I told him they died, but he has that effect on people. And he's right about the pain. It's like old, deep pain that's so far down the abyss that nothing can reach it—except maybe him. He always knows the right thing to say. He seems to be able to fix me, and I want to be fixed. All of us are just trying to do our best, after all.

I felt so low after hearing about Matisse that I decided to have a drink for the first time. Now I know why Claude is such a lush. Maybe he's onto something. Self-medicating does seem to help. It helps with sleeping, and allows me to forget all the things I don't want to remember.

February 1990

Laissez les bon temps rouler means "Let the good times roll." It's the unofficial slogan of a place that's a fondue pot full of community, cuisine, architecture, art, nature, and magic. The food in Louisiana is unbelievable. The legends you've heard are all true. If you're a food enthusiast, then why aren't you here yet? Even the biggest food critics in D.C. pay homage to New Orleans. Artists come in all different genres, and this is where the food artists flock. Recipes are born here. Dishes like blackened redfish, crawfish etouffée, jambalaya, shrimp creole, gumbo with Andouille sausage, Natchitoches meat pies, and soft shell crab, to name a few. I've been eating a lot of crawfish, fried oyster po-boy sandwiches, and red beans with rice.

Gumbeaux is open late, and it's become like a second home. I spend hours there, sitting at an outside table and drawing. A customer remarked the other day, "Gumbeaux is the spiritual hub of my life." Maybe not for all, but it's absolutely a place you can sit outside all day in perfect comfort, weather permitting. The locals say that if you stick around there long enough, you see the whole town go by from the mayor to the mailman. I enjoy sitting on the patio with a book and a bottle of wine. Hemingway was right. A bottle of wine is very good company.

One of the waitresses at Gumbeaux likes to play with fire-literally. Her name is Kandace, and she is able to manipulate strands of metal threaded from her fingers. She does this with lit steel wool balls on the end, so it looks like she's juggling fire. Her tools are gloves, Velcro, metal wires, and steel wool. They call it fire poi spinning in Hawaii, from what I understand. It appears as though she's doing tricks with yo-yos covered in flames. A gorgeous woman juggling fire twenty-four inches from her fingertips. What a show! Because the black backdrop of the night camouflages the cables, the only visible effect is of a winning silhouette and fire balloons the size of tennis balls swirling and soaring through the dark, cool air. On Friday nights, she'll do shows on the patio outside. The customers love it. We all do.

The Gumbeaux night supervisor (Sue Bell) asked if I needed a job. She said they were looking for day shift girls and that I would really fit in. She brought me an application with an alligator watermark on it. It's always nice to be recruited. All the people in Louisiana have been very warm and welcoming. I've really embraced my new home and love it here. Simplicity of heart and a desire to have a good time with good people is simply its own invitation. How can you help from loving a place like that? It's not the pretentious life I've known, among people who want to peruse your resume before deciding whether or not to even speak to you.

March 1990

Spring has sprung in Bayou Bend. The college campus looks like one big, enchanted garden. You've never seen so many flowered trees and bushes. It's like walking through Monet's garden at Giverny.

I've spent a lot of time with George over the past few months. Lots of times we drive out to his parents' house. Well, it's not so much a house as a plantation home out in the country. The Graves family is comprised of one Southern character after another. They live in Sweetwater, a really small town about twenty-five minutes north of Bayou Bend. The Graves family has the only two-story house in Sweetwater. This ostentation alone causes them to be considered terribly well-to-do among the neighboring families. They are the epitome of Southern hospitality.

George's Mom spends her time doing community works for the Junior League, cooking fabulous meals from scratch and gearing up for their annual holiday party. George's father is a strappy, stoic gentleman and a strong male figurehead. When he's nowhere to be seen, one might find him riding a horse around his property, overseeing with a cell phone in hand. He might also be teaching one of his very young nephews to drive a tractor, much to his wife's chagrin. His absolute favorite activity is flying his crop duster over his farm. He's completely unauthorized to do this and has had no formal training whatsoever.

The Graves home is a haven with a huge, expansive backyard outfitted with porch swings. There's a golden pond with ducks, fresh water mullet, turtles, and plenty of room to throw shindigs of any kind. The whole family loves to entertain. One night George and I made a bonfire and stayed up all night telling each other ghost stories. We drank hot chocolate and stared up at the stars. Life in Sweetwater is easy, slow-paced, and family oriented.

Recently George and I were driving to Lake Beatrice, and what to our wandering eyes did appear? What had to be the biggest Confederate flag in the entire world, flying right off the interstate. I almost drove off the road. It had to be like fifty feet long. This must be what people mean when they say, "The South will rise again." George said, "Yeah, that's been up for several years now. When it went up, it was kind of a controversy." George then went on to tell me about how the Confederacy was still a big deal in Bayou Bend. He said that there were Civil War re-enactments done around town, and that one of the school fraternities had an annual party called 'Southern Comfort' where everyone wore antebellum costumes and rode to the dance on horseback. The women wore southern belle ball gowns and the men dressed as soldiers. He said the girls were pretty drunk by the time the guys picked them up, and that we should definitely observe next time. He said at least two girls fall off the horses every year. We'd better make sure there's film in the camera.

March 1990

Claude must feel bad about how much he sucks because he sent me a new car last week. It arrived while I was in art class. He had one of his bimbos drive it over to the school to surprise me. The car was a gorgeous Mercedes convertible, and it was not entry level.

I learned long ago that Claude's gifts have many strings attached. He is the kind of person who will lord things over you forever. I told the driver thank you very much, but I couldn't accept. The dumbfounded driver drove away, presumably back to her regular job as a hooker. God knows where he finds these people.

I turned around to go back to class. Dr. Landry had been watching the delivery unfold out the window. As I nonchalantly walked back to my drawing, Dr. Landry asked, "Who are you?"

There was no meeting his eyes, smoldering green lanterns that they were. "No one from nowhere," I responded quietly, and picked up my eraser.

March 1990

I went to New Orleans recently and got a little out of hand at a festival. The last thing I remember is singing Jimmy Buffet songs at a piano bar and imbibing a drink that was shaped like a grenade. It's all kind of a blur. The next morning I promised George I was never drinking again. That lasted about three days.

Between my self-medicating and having what could be easily mistaken for having a good time, my lack of organization has become a problem. I even forgot to attend the annual scholarship dinner. The elderly couple that pays for the scholarship sat there for an hour, waiting for me to show up.

Dr. Landry met me for coffee, and I asked him how to handcraft a sincere apology. He said that would be the polite thing to do, but it wouldn't do any good. He said the elderly couple yanked my scholarship. They wanted to give it to someone who "consistently fulfilled their obligations." Dr. Landry said this had been embarrassing for him, since he had gone to them on my behalf in the first place and asked them to help me. It made me feel really low, to have disappointed him.

Maybe I should look into that waitressing job at Gumbeaux. I'm there all the time anyway, might was well be getting paid for it.

3 GUMBEAUX

April 1990

    Gumbeaux **restaurant is** owned by a local married couple, Bubba and Lulu Bettencourt. Lulu manages the café and day shift. Bubba manages the bar and night shift. They may be a married couple, but they're nothing alike. Lulu is very religious. She is all about being a Southern Baptist and doesn't seem to have a sense of humor. She spends most of her time in the back office balancing the books.

    On the flip side of the spectrum, we have her husband Bubba, who oversees the night shift. Bubba stands next to the beer keg all evening, cup in hand (we only sell Louisiana beers, like Dixie and Blackened Voodoo). He says he only has one drink per shift, but he "just refreshes it from time to time." Bubba is gracious and polite, the customers enjoy him very much, and he gets to basically hang out with friends each night. He doesn't have much of an assistant manager working nights for him. Her name is Sue Bell, and she's a piece of work. It's a challenge to actually find her, as she is constantly on a smoke break. Every time you walk by her, she's saying something really bizarre, usually to a customer. Some examples are "I feed my houseplants nothing but beer and whiskey," "I look rode hard and put up wet before I have my first cup of coffee," "I GAR-ON-TEE you will love it," "It's six, one half dozen or the other," "I'm fixin' ta get to it," "The cheese done slid off my cracker," and "So there I was, waterskiing naked on Lake Bistineau."

    Sue Bell has a sister who comes to see her at least once a month. It looks like she might be pregnant, which is odd since she has to be at least fifty. The cash register is always a bit off on Sue Bell's watch. Bubba apparently doesn't care. I'll bet his wife does, though. Each day at 3 p.m., Bubba shows up and meets with Lulu in the back office. They go over the receipts, discuss the issues of the day and sometimes you can hear them yelling at each other through the door. Then Lulu storms out, slams the front door and screeches off in her Chrysler LeBaron convertible.

All the waitresses are hot college girls, except for Sue Bell, who's like fifty and monitors the appearance of the staff with the scrutiny of a madam. It must work because they look fantastic. I work the day shift. All the girls on the day shift are clean cut and cute. Cheerleader types. We have one girl who was second runner up for Miss Bayou Bend. Apparently you don't get much for second runner up. You get to work at Gumbeaux and have customers drool over you. Our uniforms are pretty cute. The day staff wears white T-shirts, the night staff wears black. All the waitresses are white. Everyone on the kitchen staff is black: the cooks, busboys, and kitchen managers. Not sure what's up with that, but that's the way it is. The three non-waitresses I have bonded with somewhat are Willie the oyster shucker and lead bartender, Catherine the head chef, and Clarence who busses tables for the lunch shift.

Gumbeaux is a very fun place to work. We have a lot of regular customers who know us by name and have their favorites. For instance, there is a group of six old men who play golf every Tuesday, then come to have lunch with us afterwards. They leave a dollar each and like lots of iced tea with lemon. The professors from Audubon College come there a lot, too. Mr. Fitzgerald, the director from the theatre department, came in by himself today and wanted to sit in my section. I brought him a coffee with chicory and a side of steaming, frothy milk. He drank one sip, shook his head, grinned, and said, "That'll put some lead in your pencil." He was sitting under a framed poster for Mardi Gras, 1975.

George and some guy he knows were sitting by the window, looking over at a house near the college. They were making snide comments about the new owners and their decorating skills.

"Lordy, would you look at that?" George remarked.

"There should be a city ordinance against tackiness of that magnitude. Elect me; you won't even have to pay me. It's a civic duty," agreed the friend.

"It used to be such a cute house. Look. Look what they did to it. Can you see the gazebo from where you're sitting? What's wrong with a white gazebo? Why did they have to go with pink?" George pointed out the window, quite indignant.

His friend shook his head in mutual disappointment and stirred his lobster bisque. "Really? One Venus di Milo statue wasn't enough? They had to have two?"

George looked around and whispered in what he probably thought was a discreet voice, "I'm all for representing, but look at all the rainbow stickers on their cars. Lesbians always overdo it. Don't you think so?"

"Oh no," laughed his dining companion. "You're on your own with that opinion, you homophobic bastard."

George doesn't say effeminate things in front of his family. They have no idea he likes men as opposed to women. He hasn't told them. They wouldn't be down with it at all. His father would disown him for sure. He says his mother might already have an idea, but is very much of the 'don't ask, don't tell' mindset.

Before my shift ended, I took a big bag of trash out to the dumpster. On top of the dumpster was the biggest, blackest crow you ever saw in your life. He was just parked there, staring at me. Even when I got close, he didn't move. He just stared at me. His harvest moon yellow eyes were the only part of him that wasn't shiny blue black. I threw away my trash and went back inside. The bird and I just watched each other the whole time. Neither of us made a sound.

May 1990

Yesterday, a couple of the Gumbeaux girls gave me a makeover. It started off at the local cosmetology school. When you don't have a lot of money, you get creative with what you've got. One of the girls told me that I looked like Bettie Page, and I should blow that look up more. First, we changed my hair color to a shade called 'Black Dahlia.' Then, we experimented with pale powder-based makeup and candy apple red lipstick. They did my nails and took me shopping at a vintage clothes store in the French Quarter. Lots of 1950's style accessories and voila—a whole new look. Easy as pie.

I saw Dr. Landry in the school cafeteria not long ago. You could tell he found my new look distracting, because he was staring at me and walked into a wall. Dr. McNeely was with him and looked really pissed. She said something I couldn't hear and then whacked him with the backside of her cafeteria tray.

Clarence, Willie, and Catherine liked my makeover. Clarence said, "Very nice job. Those girls really got a hold of you; it's a big difference. You could even probably pass for high yaller." I don't know what that's supposed to mean, but it sure made Catherine and Willie go into hysterics. They are both very overweight and convulsed all over the place from laughter. I asked the next customer who walked in the door what "high yaller" meant. She looked highly offended and walked right back out of the restaurant. Guess it's a sensitive topic for some reason. Clarence saw all of this go down. He pointed and laughed and told me I was the worst waitress ever.

May 1990

Louisiana is one adventure after another. George and I just got back from Venice, Louisiana. George's father had purchased a fishing trip for him. He assumed his son would appreciate a fishing trip for his birthday. He sure doesn't know his kid too well. Mr. Graves probably imagined George would want to take a male friend along, but he wanted to take me. My parents had taken me fishing from time to time, but just for trout. Today we hunted big fish, like *Old Man and the Sea* big fish. Tuna, mahi-mahi, tarpon, marlin, and red snapper. I wasn't too interested until George showed me a picture of a red snapper. The fish was the most incredible shade of red. Was that picture touched up? No? Well, that would be something to see.

Venice is about seventy-five miles south of New Orleans. It's where the Mississippi River spills into the Gulf of Mexico. I asked the guy at the register where we signed up for the fishing boat how such big sea fish could be found so close to shore. He said that Venice had unusual proximity to deep, deep water, and that the Mississippi River fed nutrients into the local area. The offshore oil rig platforms created an artificial reef for the fish. Our fishing guide walked out. He introduced himself as Huey. George and I agreed he was handsome in a Cajun Man kind of way. Huey loaded us onto his boat, a mid-sized catamaran. He asked if we had brought suntan lotion, Dramamine, towels, hats, fishing licenses, ice chests to load the fish in, rubber boots, and cameras. We had. "Then let's go get you guys a yellow fin," Huey smiled at us and helped me onto the boat.

Huey seemed to be getting a kick out of our wardrobe selections for the outing. I was wearing a white bikini top with red polka dots and white short shorts, like a 1940s pin-up girl. George was decked out like Thurston Howell III from *Gilligan's Island.*

"Look at the shark," Huey remarked out of nowhere, pointing towards the bow of the boat. George and I both screamed and clung to each other for dear life. He rolled his eyes. "It's just a whale shark. Loosen up. He's just saying hi." Huey looked pretty disgusted and sort of conjured up memories of the crusty shark hunter in *Jaws.*

We ended up catching a forty-pound amberjack. Of course Huey did most of the work while George and I stood around slack jawed. It's wonderful being on the water, out at sea. When you see the American flag waving recklessly in the breeze, defiantly flapping, it looks like what freedom feels like.

There's no other feeling like riding on a boat. The water was still, like a great lake, and the catamaran sliced through the water with the precision of a knife through ganache. Lying on the bow of the boat in the sunshine was heavenly. Eyes closed, listening to the engine, feeling an occasional spray of mist. George tapped my shoulder and pointed. There were dolphins swimming alongside the boat. They were surfing our current. They were dodging and playing not just alongside the boat, but in front of the boat. The boat could have easily run them over, but the confidence of the dolphins was amazing. They were solid muscle and incredibly athletic, playing in the waves and having a ball. We were exhausted at the end of the day, and George went home with his prized catch to show off for his father. The colors which comprised the fish's scaly body were truly amazing. Granddad once told me that the greatest artists were inspired by nature, inspired by the creations of God.

May 1990

I accidentally crossed a line in the sands of acceptability with Dr. Landry. I was in his office, and the conversation started well enough. I asked him what it meant if Clarence called me "high yaller." He laughed so hard he started choking. Somehow the conversation eventually digressed to my observation that Audubon wasn't a real school because it didn't offer pre-law.

"All right. That's enough out of you, Veronica." Dr. Landry's eyes flashed and he looked like a Doberman about to take down a burglar. "You're completely out of line. I will not sit here and listen to you badmouth Audubon College like that. I'm the head of the art department, in case you forgot. I see how you are. You don't commit to anything. You're not that good of a student. You're anti-establishment and anti-community. You're not in a sorority, you don't go to the art club meetings, and you're not on any of the teams. It's easier for you to dump on things and criticize them, as opposed to actually doing something. You insist on being against everything, but at some point you have to be for something. So don't ever let me hear you badmouth the college again because I will be compelled to stop you from doing so. You may not like the way I do it, either." He was really hot under the collar. He was pointing at me, too. He had his finger in my face and everything.

I had never seen him lose his cool and was kind of impressed, actually. "I'm sorry, Dr. Landry," I apologized. "I didn't mean to say anything bad about the school. Please forgive me."

That diffused him. His face returned to normal person color. "I forgave you before you even asked. But you were out of line. It really is shocking about how entitled your generation is, though."

"That makes you sound a hundred years old," I said very softly, hoping he didn't get offended again.

He pushed aside a huge stack of magazines so he could see me better. A bunch of them fell over, but he didn't seem to notice or care. "Maybe I am old. But that doesn't mean I don't have people benched that want to come to this game." He meant himself. He was the game.

"Oh, like who?" I asked. "Dr. McNeely, right? I've seen you have lunch together in the cafeteria."

"She's an alternate. And it sounds like someone's paying attention," he grinned, running a hand absently through his hair.

"I'm sorry for what I said about the school," I apologized again.

"I'm sorry that I called you a royal pain in the ass," Dr. Landry apologized in return.

"You never called me a royal pain in the ass!" I cried.

"Well, I have now." He drummed his pencil for a while on his desk. "All kidding aside, there's something I need to ask you about. I got a call today from the Kimbell Museum in Fort Worth, Texas. They called asking for Mary Fey. Not Veronica – Mary. They said they had heard that Mary Fey was studying art here, so the call got transferred to my assistant."

"Yeah, I don't know, sounds like a wrong number." Since Fait and Fey sound exactly the same, Dr. Landry wasn't making the connection, thank God. He waited a bit for me to confess willingly, which of course did not happen.

He locked eyes with me from three inches away—even his breath was fantastic—and said, "They asked my assistant to pass on a message to Mary Fey. They would like to talk with her or her uncle about some kind of a loan, whatever that means."

"Really?" I don't have much of a poker face. Hopefully the horror on my face looked like surprise.

"Really." He folded his arms across his chest and waited for an explanation. Ten seconds of this stare down contest felt like ten minutes.

"Well, that had to be a misunderstanding. Right, Dr. Landry?" I smiled brightly, but he frowned in return. He wasn't buying it. I've tried to cover my tracks but all you can do is all you can do.

"Is there anything you would like to tell me?" He was giving me one more chance to come clean. I just shrugged and asked him what was up with the Spanish Inquisition. He exhaled in irritation, put his glasses on and sat down at his desk, indicating that the exchange was over.

I left Dr. Landry's office. Walking down the hall, there was a big framed photo of him and one of his professor friends in their convocation robes. The robes had velvet trim and were ornamented with different colors. The colors were coded to their areas of study, probably. They looked kind of like religious robes. Preachers or teachers; they could pass for either.

Dr. Landry was there smiling at the camera. It was a great photo of him. I stared at it and wondered if I sat on his lap and whispered to him how sorry I was, if he would like that. If I kissed him, would he like that? I imagined him saying, "No, you didn't do that well enough. We're going to have to try again." I imagined Dr. McNeely coming in and screaming.

The fog of my fantasy world evaporated when I realized Dr. Landry had come out into the hall to get some coffee. He had busted me looking at his picture. I got all flustered and tried to look nonchalant. "See anything you like?" he asked softly, trying not to laugh. My sense of urgency to leave spiked and it was like swimming against a psychological gulf stream.

It's terrible to be afraid of what you want most. If only courage could be bottled and sold.

July 1990

You know, it's really hot here. I didn't realize how hot heat can be. They failed to mention it in the recruiting brochures. They must schedule the visits during the most fabulous times of the year; it wasn't like this when we first came down. It is oppressive heat that sits like a three-hundred-pound man on your chest. So humid and thick you can barely breathe. Not all the time, but sometimes. Like, now. I've been taking ice cubes and running them all over my body. From the time I left to dorm yesterday to getting into my car, my sleek and polished hairdo turned into a frizzy nightmare. Betty says that's why aerosol hairspray was invented, but when I tried it, it looked all stiff and crunchy. Perhaps this is why perms seem to be such a hit with the sorority set.

School is out for summer, but they are letting me stay in the dorm. I miss Dr. Landry, who's taken a group of students to Paris. He says he'll find any excuse to get to Paris. I would have liked to have gone, but wasn't about to ask Claude for the money.

September 1990

George drove me to a cotton field that was actually within town. There were rows of restaurants, a school, and then boom— several acres of cotton fields. He said that the farmers weren't ready to sell out to Bennigan's or whoever just yet. We pulled over and walked through the cotton fields. When you broke open a pod, there was fluffy cotton inside. I stroked a pod against my face and got scratched.

"Ouch!" I shrieked.

"You have to take the seeds out, Veronica. You've heard of Eli Whitney and the cotton gin, have you not?" George sighed with feigned annoyance.

"It's really hard work getting these out," I whined.

"Right, Genius," George agreed. "It's almost as if you'd have to have slaves to do it."

"You should be nicer to me, and I'll remember you in my will," I told George.

"Yeah, that and ten cents should buy me a bag of chips," he laughed.

Sitting there in the cotton field was very strange. I didn't know how to feel, but it was definitely unsettling. You could imagine all the poor slaves from years back tilling this field. That seemed like a million years ago, but the field was still there, right in the middle of town. It wasn't as long ago as you might think. The past was colliding with the present. You couldn't just act like nothing had happened. Man's inhumanity to man had taken place there and the proof surrounded us on all sides.

September 1990

I just had my first art showing. It was a night of high highs and low lows. The showing was for a series of oversized flowers. All acrylic on canvas, colors unblended. I had fifteen paintings up, filling an entire room in the college museum. The school had helped me promote it. Dr. Landry's staff had put out fliers and had the docents invite alumni. They had put forth quite an effort to make my showing a big event. There were five hundred silver balloons, waiters carrying around fancy cheese trays and even multiple wine stations. If you came in off the street and didn't know better, you'd think you were viewing the work of a successful working artist. There were little placards next to each piece, and the prices averaged $250.00 per painting. One was a bouquet of pink peonies, set in a wooden frame from one of the incredible antique stores on Royal Street in the French Quarter. That one was $650.00. It was my piece de resistance or whatever.

I wore a little red cocktail dress, which you would say was classy with a pinch of sexy thrown in for good measure. A ton of people showed up, and they were saying things like, "new painter on the scene", "she's only a freshman", and similar comments. I walked up on several people who didn't know that I was the artist and listened to their conversations. Everyone seemed to be pretty positive, except for one tall, well-dressed, somewhat snooty man who said my style was only appropriate to hang in fast food restaurants. What a bastard! I almost choked on my champagne upon hearing that one. Most people have the decency to wait until they leave the event, but you can't win them all. At least, that's what Granddad used to say.

Someone tapped me on the shoulder halfway through the event and I almost had a heart attack when I saw it was Claude. No warning whatsoever. I never told him about the art showing. He was wearing his favorite Armani suit but had clearly spilled mustard all over the front of it. "Hi Mary." He was a little wobbly and smelled like he'd been swimming in a septic tank.

"Claude. I wasn't expecting you to come. What are you doing here?" I hastily folded my arms in front of my chest to camouflage my cleavage. It didn't stop him from staring, though.

"Nice way to greet your uncle. Where's my hug?" He reached out for an embrace and I let him hug me. He hugged me longer than was necessary, which struck me as suggestive and nauseating. I did not hug him back and managed to avoid getting covered in mustard. "Listen," he said, appraising me in my dress and heels, "I need your help. I need you to come with me."

The sense of urgency in his voice worried me. "What? Right now? Why? Is Grandma okay?"

He looked taken aback. "Um, yeah, I guess. I should probably have someone check. Anyhow, there are some people at the Getty who are interested in a partnership with us. It's going to be a trade arrangement. I need you to go with me to Malibu. I've got the jet waiting for us, so we need to get moving." He looked around, eyes squinting with impatience. "Who do you have to bang to get a drink around here? Anyway, this thing with the Getty could be a very cool joint venture for us. You'll love it."

It made me so upset that he just showed up like that. He must have heard I was happy and had to put a stop to it. He had to have known about this, it couldn't possibly be a coincidence that he was here during my art opening. He was almost acting like it wasn't really going on, like he was trying to ignore all the people and all the paintings.

"Claude, I'm actually a little busy right now. Look around you. I'm doing a joint venture with *myself.*" I swept my arm across the room at paintings, the people and the party.

"That doesn't make sense," he responded, a little confused.

"This night is a really big deal for me. The school advertised it and everything. All these people are here to see my work, so I can't just walk out of here right now to jump on a plane with you." It sure would have been nice if he had just come to celebrate with me, like a normal relative. Assuming that's how normal relatives even act. I wouldn't know.

"Well, going to the Getty with you has been on my schedule for a while. I must have mentioned it but maybe we didn't schedule it formally," he slurred. "I wasn't aware of how glamorous you are now."

"Whatever." I started to walk away from him.

Claude grabbed my arm and pulled me back. "I heard you lost your scholarships."

I asked how he had heard that. He blamed it on the grapevine. He's always blaming everything on the stupid grapevine. I wouldn't be surprised if he has someone spying on me.

His face was smug and his chest was all puffed up like a toad. "I thought you might be ready to come home to D.C., and we can just forget about the recent unpleasantness between us." He smiled grandly, as if bestowing a huge favor.

"Recent?" I snarled, furious upon seeing the smug smile on his red, swollen face. The unpleasantness between us is not recent. It's been unpleasant for years!" Just calling it like it is.

That angered him. "Mary, it's time for you to come home. I've indulged this whim of yours about as long as I can." His eyes looked really cold and all of a sudden I felt like a scared little kid.

"Why can't you just be happy for me?" I asked, choking back a sob. I was mad at myself for letting him get to me. "Why can't you just be proud of me? I don't want to leave. I like it here. Besides, this is a four-year program. I can't just drop out," I protested.

Claude groaned in exasperation. "We're *rich*, Mary. We can do whatever the hell we want. Besides, four years is just too long." He seemed to be breathing kind of hard, as if he'd been jogging through the parking lot. He's no athlete, that's for sure.

"Too long for whom?" I wanted to know.

"It's hard fundraising without you there," Claude explained. "I can't do it without you. You're my ace in the hole, my lucky charm. Ever since you've been gone, it's just not the same." He tried to touch my hair and I smacked his hand away.

"I'm not your genie, Claude. You can't just show up, rub the bottle and expect me to do whatever you want. You're going to have to make your own magic from now on."

He wobbled a bit, and then drunkenly peered around the room. "You're not a genie, you're an artist. You wanted to be an artist so you came to *Louisiana*. Who do you think you are? Do you think you're going to be just like Dad? Well, you're not. I'm not and you're not. Neither of us is good enough to even bother trying. You'll never be as good as he was, so what's the point? You should be home with me promoting his legacy." He stopped a food attendant and took several mini cheesecakes from a platter. He stuffed them in his mouth all at once, and raspberry sauce began to trickle from the corners of his mouth. He resembled a drunk, slightly overweight vampire (with a penchant for mustard and Armani).

"It's my life too, Claude. Don't try to make this into a tragedy. There is nothing wrong with my wanting to attend college. You can't make me feel guilty about this." But he was absolutely making me feel guilty. He was playing the 'Don't you love Granddad?' card. He really knows how to turn the screws and upset me, and he loves drama.

"Our lives aren't as important as his legacy, don't you get it? We are all that is left of the Fait family. You have abandoned your station!" He gave off a huge belch that could have won contests of that nature all over the country. "You had to come down here and play artist. A princess like you came down here to the end of the world to go slumming. I would never have believed it."

Again, with the princess comments! I serve crawfish pies to people and go home after each shift smelling like fried shrimp. There's nothing princessy about that. I told him, "I disagree with you. You don't know what you're talking about. It's been great here. The people are wonderful, the town is beautiful and the food is incredible."

"You're waiting tables in a Cajun restaurant, right?" he asked, like he already knew for sure.

"Yes, that's right." Doesn't it sound like he could be having me followed? Or is that just paranoia talking?

"Unbelievable. You've never had a job in your life!" He motioned at a waiter to come to him. The waiter could see that Claude didn't really need any more drinks and ignored the request.

"You never let me *have* a job," I reminded him.

"But why are you waiting tables?" He wanted to know. "That's disgusting. It's scary down here. They have snakes that can eat a person whole, I read about it. I hear you can get yellow fever in the swamps. Yellow fever, Mary. Now, that is serious." Claude grabbed a beverage from a passing tray, practically knocking over the waiter in the process. He was really tanked.

"Please don't call me Mary when we're here, Claude. I'm supposed to be going by my middle name, remember?" I glanced around the room, hoping no one had heard him.

"Going from Mary to Veronica. Different name, different look. You do look different, that's for sure. That dress makes you look like a hooker. It might give people the wrong idea. That's probably not the way you want to get recognized as an artist. Or is it?" Claude started twisting my arm, and it hurt. I asked him to let go. He was getting a little loud. A man suddenly appeared on my right. He was around my age, and I think of myself as a girl—but he definitely wasn't a boy. He was a man, very muscular, darkly attractive and it seemed like he was the bouncer. He was wearing a dress shirt like all the other guests at the opening, but his *Hello My Name is* name badge just had the word 'Ninja' written on it in bold red letters. "Excuse me, miss?" The alleged ninja inquired in a deliciously sexy southern drawl. "Is this man bothering you?"

"Hey, jackass, mind your business," was Claude's eloquent reply.

"What did you say?" The ninja asked, verifying that he had in fact been insulted. His cobalt blue eyes narrowed, almost obscured by thick black lashes. His hair was onyx colored and fell unkempt around his face, like a dark halo.

"You heard me," my uncle sneered.

The ninja grabbed him and threw him against the wall. I **gasped a little and started to feel really good.** The ninja gave me a quick glace to ensure I wasn't going to freak out or anything, then he pressed Claude's face into the bricks with astonishing speed and precision. It was all I could do to refrain from bursting into applause. I have literally been wishing something like this would happen for as long as I can remember.

"It's between me and her," Claude answered as best he could, as his lips were squashed together and his teeth were up against the brick wall.

"You calling me a jackass *makes* it my business," the ninja told him in a calm voice that sounded like it was having a good time. "So now you can apologize to me, and to this beautiful lady right here." The ninja winked at me sexily. I felt a little faint. This was so delightful and so unexpected.

"Are you crazy? I'm not apologizing to you!" yelled Claude, drawing attention from other attendees.

The ninja smacked him across the face. No one ever dares even look at Claude wrong back in D.C., but his money is no good here in Bayou Bend. I was excited and glowing. Claude was about to get his ass kicked and I wasn't directly responsible. "I don't want to have to ask you again," warned the hero. A small crowd had gathered to watch, but no one seemed interested in breaking it up. In fact, I could hear bets being placed regarding the outcome of this exchange.

"Fine," Claude agreed unhappily. "I'm sorry." The ninja released him with a bounce against the wall. Claude gave me a horrible look to confirm that this wasn't over, and left the party. He probably went back to the airport. He flew twenty-five hundred miles just to ruin my night. My red cocktail dress, cherished an hour earlier, now made me feel really sleazy.

I thought maybe I could get a second opinion on that, but before I could address the ninja, he was dragged off by a possessive brunette. He apparently already has a special lady friend. She came out of nowhere and was glaring angrily at me. I hadn't even done anything yet. He smiled at me and left. I didn't get his real name. There is no way anyone actually has the name 'Ninja'. He was the only guy aside from Dr. Landry who has made alarms go off in my head so far. It was a shame he had to go.

I went outside and looked at all the beautiful twinkle lights that had been hung in the oak trees. The weather was perfect. It was late September and fall was closing in on Indian summer. An owl sounded off in a tree, and his hoot-hoot-hoot call seemed the loneliest of all sounds. Even though Claude was gone and had been bested by my ninja friend, it was still disparaging. What had started off as a wonderful evening had been destroyed. Claude killed it. I was crying the stoic cry of trying not to cry—you know the one. Then, poof—Dr. Landry appeared by my side.

"Miss Veronica? What are you doing out here? You're neglecting your fan club." I'd never seen him in a suit before; it was a very flattering charcoal gray number, complete with a pomegranate red tie and white brushed-cotton shirt. I resisted a strong impulse to run my fingers across the fabric. Just to see what it felt like, of course.

"I just wanted some air." I tried not to look upset, and smiled warmly like life was one big garden party after another. That's what these southern girls do; that's the secret. I figured it out one day while in attendance of the Miss Sweetwater Beauty Pageant (George made me go). People can say what they please about southern belles, but I find them fascinating and brilliant. Statistics don't lie. Those girls know how to win them some pageants. You can look it up.

In contrast to my melancholy, Dr. Landry was animated and upbeat. "Some air, yeah. It's nice out. Listen, I came out here to give you some great news. We just got a call at the reception desk from someone wants to buy your whole collection. Since he's buying it all, it's fairly standard for you to make him a deal. The gallery typically takes twenty percent but they're waiving that, since you're a student." He laughed and patted me on the back. "Can you believe it? You sold every single piece in the show!" He waited for my reaction, was surprised at my stony silence and continued. "This is a big deal, Veronica. No student here has ever sold out like this at their first show. Most students don't manage to sell art like this. In fact, most artists don't manage to sell art like this."

My focus began to lose its viselike grip on Claude and shift towards the present. Someone had really bought all my paintings? Were they even good? Did the buyer have bad taste or was I actually talented? The truth was probably somewhere in between. I had been petrified about displaying my paintings for the whole world to see. I had never felt so exposed, like a patient etherized upon a table. Dr. Landry advises doing things that scare you each day, so that you can continually become braver and braver. I do want him to think that I'm brave, so when he asked me to display my paintings, I said yes.

His approval means a lot to me. "They all sold? Really?" I choked back a sob. I must have looked pretty pathetic, because Dr. Landry took out a tissue and started grooming me a bit.

"Really. I can't understand how you could possibly be upset under the circumstances. And you have mascara running down your face. You don't want all these people to see you like this, right? Put your game face on and we'll find you even more sponsors. Artists need sponsors. Can you imagine where your career could go if you had the Medici family at your disposal?" He was trying to make me laugh. I tried to accommodate him but the laugh wouldn't come out. He studied me as if trying to diagnose my symptoms. "What happened? Was it your uncle?"

He doesn't miss much. "Yes, it was Claude, all right. He really upset me," I admitted. His comments were to my hurt feelings as aloe vera is to a sunburn.

"He came down to see your show. That's nice, right?" Dr. Landry has a tendency to assign positive qualities to people who don't deserve them. I guess noble people want to believe everyone else is noble too. They must not know that they're almost extinct, like Komodo dragons.

"Claude said I look like a hooker in this dress," I sobbed. "I thought it looked okay, but it was really upsetting. Why would he say something like that to me?"

"What?" cried Dr. Landry. "That's ridiculous. You look incredibly elegant and un-hooker-like in any way. He was obviously *trying* to upset you. You don't know how beautiful you are. You don't see the way people look at you."

I could feel myself blushing. Had he really just said I was beautiful? It was hard to even respond. "Nobody's looking at me."

"That's what you think. You can't see it; you're too busy focusing on being invisible," he told me. "But like it or not, you are absolutely stunning."

Something in his smile made me feel like I had vertigo. Time to change the subject before I lost my head completely and confessed my stupid crush. "Thank you. Sorry to be so upset, but Claude has that effect on me. I thought I wouldn't have to see him again for a while because home is twenty-five hundred miles away."

Dr. Landry shook his head. "You can't escape the past, even if home is twenty-five thousand miles away," he informed me.

A tsunami wave of anger rose, and I threw my champagne glass so it smashed against the wall. "I should have killed that bastard years ago. It would be doing the world a good deed, but I don't have the guts to take him out. I'm too scared about getting caught and going to jail."

He glanced around to make sure no one had overhead the death threat. "I will deny this conversation took place if you ever succeed. But go on." He didn't like what I was saying, but at least he kept listening.

"It just sucks, you know? Tonight, I was at my *best*. I can't look any better than I did. I can't be any more charming than I was. I'll probably never sell all my paintings in one night again. And he doesn't care. It doesn't matter. Even at my absolute best, he doesn't think I'm good enough."

Dr. Landry remained quiet for a while. There was no sound but my sobbing and a few crickets. Then he gently touched my face so I had to make eye contact with him and said, "Listen to me. I get that you're trying to make your own way in the world, without riding your family's coat tails. That's noble. You were wise to get away from your uncle. He's not a good role model for you. But don't base your perceptions of men off of Claude. He puts conditions on you. You don't want a guy who only loves you at your best. That's going to set you up for failure. No one can sustain being at the top of his or her game twenty-four/seven. You want a guy who loves you at your worst. Who adores you and wants to take care of you when things are bad, not just good. You want a guy who takes care of you when you're sick, makes you chicken soup when you can hardly get out of bed, and who holds your hair back when you have to throw up. You want a guy who loves you at your worst. Not at your best. It's easy to love someone at their best. Do you understand?"

I understood completely and felt better immediately. Being in his presence was better than a drug. I gave him a big hug and whispered "thank you" in his ear. He got flustered and started cleaning his glasses with a cocktail napkin. "We'd better get back to the party," he said, and then he disappeared for rest of the night.

When the show was over, I walked barefoot across campus carrying my shoes. All the other students were carefully nestled all snug in their beds and I had the campus to myself. When I crossed the bridge over the pond, there was a group of fireflies on the other side. They hovered around my head for a moment and then flickered further and further away. They were like electric butterflies, punching holes in the nighttime. It's going to be hard to paint that image, but maybe I'll give it a go.

September 1990

For this next breaking news bulletin, you might want to sit down. This stuff is freaking crazy. George took me to a drive-thru place around the corner that sells thirty-two oz. daiquiris to go. Yes, you read that right. The place we went to is called Lagniappe Daiquiri and used to be a gas station. I asked the drink attendant how they can get away with selling margaritas and piña coladas like that. The drink attendant slapped a tiny piece of tape over the hole where the straw goes in the lid and said, "Now, it ain't an open container, darlin'. You be sure to come back for another round, hear?" George laughed at my shocked expression as she took the order for the next customer, who wanted an extra shot of 151 in his drink.

I'm so over living in the dorm. We have these four exchange students from Thailand down the hall from us. They're always cooking and the food smells incredible. Every time I go by and ask if they're cooking, they deny it. It's the best panang you've ever smelled. This week I'll get to escape that exquisite torture for one of a different sort. I'm house-sitting for Dr. Landry. I was surprised that he asked me. This went down at Gumbeaux. I was about to leave, but Dr. Landry materialized before me out of nowhere.

He greeted me warmly. "Hello Miss V. How's the studying?"

"Yesh." Another perfect behavioral example of how I become tongue-tied in his presence.

He carried on as if I had said something routine and articulate. "Would you be able to do some house-sitting for me the first weekend in October? I'm going out of town and I was wondering if you'd watch my place. I'd pay you $100.00 for your trouble."

"I can do that," I easily agreed. "Do you want me to stay there?" The possibilities were already sending my mind reeling.

"You're welcome to do so, if you want. But if you'd at least pick up the mail and newspapers and make sure no one sets it on fire that would be wonderful. I'll leave a key under the mat."

"No problem. You got it. Where will you be going?"

"To a graphic arts conference in Houston. Thank you so much. When you're there, feel free to help yourself to anything in the fridge or the bookshelves. You'll see I have nothing but books. Just don't drink that bottle of Dom Pérignon. That one I'm saving for something special."

Out the window, I watched him leave Gumbeaux to get into his Saab. He slipped comically down the stairs and then looked around to see if anyone had noticed before getting into the car. Goofball. He was so adorable.

Inside my head (a mysterious place where strange things happen) a thought began to take shape. Maybe this would be a good opportunity to seduce him. He could teach me about sex or whatever. I've never done it before and want it to be with someone wonderful. Then I had a ridiculous romantic fantasy. It took place at Dr. Landry's house, or rather my impression of what it must look like inside:

Dr. Landry comes in the kitchen to find me making crème brûlée. I am wearing nothing but a sexy French maid uniform and am holding one of those little torches.

He says, "Well, I guess I'm here just in time for dessert." No, scratch that; that is too much even for a fantasy like this. He says, "Well, hello, Miss Veronica. Is that for me?"

"The crème brûlée?"

"No. Not the crème brûlée." He grabs me and throws me down on this butcher block he's got in the kitchen. I have blackberries out so I can decorate the crème brûlée, and they are getting everywhere.

"They're going to leave marks," I say breathlessly.

"Not compared to the ones I'm going to leave."

September 1990

Took out the trash tonight. Was shocked to see that the same crow was sitting on top of the dumpster again. He was huge. He kept very still until I got close to the dumpster. Then he ruffled his feathers and cawed ferociously at me. It was terrifying. I ran back to the restaurant, trash in tow. Clarence wanted to know why I didn't throw away the trash. I told him about the crow. He said I was a sissy, and he went back to the dumpster with me. There was no crow; it had disappeared. There was no one there but me and Clarence and Clarence's smart remarks about my cowardice/sanity.

September 1990

A few of the football players from the New Orleans Saints came in the other day. Even though they've had a rough go of it, you should see how beloved they are by their fans. A few of them kept yelling, "Who dat? Who dat?" The fans have great attitudes. Of course they would like them to win the Super Bowl, but they're not fair weather fans. Not by a long shot. We posed with them for photos, and they're supposed to be in the *Times Picayune* on Sunday. One of them asked out my co-worker Betty. She's all excited and keeps asking us what she should wear.

Betty looks exactly like a Barbie doll and men typically fall all over her. She appeared in one of the *Playboy* college issues and makes sure everyone knows it. Customers actually bring copies of her photo in *Playboy* for her to sign. She's always bragging about how one day Hugh Hefner himself is going to stroll through the door and join us for muffaletta sandwiches. Betty loves her local celebrity status. Bubba loves it too. He's so proud of her. She's so fun and upbeat it's hard not to like her.

We hosted a wedding reception here at Gumbeaux the other night. It was really beautiful. The flowers, music, lighting, outfits of the bridal party—every detail was really lovely. It was a really nice wedding. I said, "You know, this is a lovely wedding," to Willie the oyster shucker and Clarence the busboy. They said weddings were lame and they wanted it to be over as soon as possible so they could go watch football at home. You can't go by their opinion, though. They don't know anything. I was discreetly drinking a Bon Vivant. That's a drink Willie invented. A Bon Vivant is like a mojito crossed with a hurricane. Amazing on a hot day. He said he created it for a customer he fell in love with last year. She was in the Junior League of Bayou Bend and used to come into Gumbeaux for drinks after playing eighteen holes of golf with the other junior leaguers. Willie said he knew he didn't stand a chance with her, but he could at least invent a drink for her as a doff of his cap.

The wedding reception had gotten to that stage where people start making speeches. The bride had a daughter from a previous marriage, about eight years old. The daughter wanted to say a few words to celebrate the occasion. In the microphone, she said how grateful she was that her new father had come into their lives. She said she was glad her mom was so happy now. A good place to stop might have been there because she had a lot on her eight-year-old mind. She went on to say that before her mother started dating her new father, things had gotten pretty bad. Mom was drinking in the daytime and she wasn't always very nice. Her bottom lip trembled dramatically, and she collapsed into inconsolable sobs to convey how bad things actually had been. The groom went to hug the little girl; the bride's eyes were big as saucers. The bride then got on the microphone to do damage control, saying that she did the best she could, and that it really was fine; it wasn't that bad. She could have strangled her daughter on the spot.

I looked back to see Willie and Clarence, laughing their asses off in the back of the restaurant. "You was right, Veronica," gasped Clarence, "This sure is a lovely wedding."

The Mayor came in recently and gave Lulu and Bubba the key to the city. He said that Gumbeaux represented Louisiana to many tourists and that we were all state ambassadors. Clarence immediately got an attitude and insisted upon being called Your Ambassadorship for weeks afterward. We received an award. Lulu was really proud of it. She took it to a framing store and had it framed and matted. Once it was done, she placed it right over the cash register, next to a company photo of the entire Gumbeaux staff. Lulu beams with pride at the award each time she comes in the door.

October 1990

A customer's kid got his head stuck in one of the chairs at Gumbeaux recently. He was being a total brat, and even though I asked his parents to stop him from running all over the restaurant, no one seemed to care but me. That is, not until he got his head stuck in the chair. Bubba was trying to get the kid's head out of the space between the seat and chair back. He had a screwdriver at first, and then moved on to a power drill. The kid was screaming, and the parents were threatening legal action unless they were somehow compensated for their inconvenience. Bubba told them that the complaint department was located fifty feet right out the door. It was their own fault for not watching their kid. We can't do it; someone's got to serve the gumbo. Spectacular gumbo at that.

Gumbo is comprised of science, art and magic. You may already know this. So many ingredients are put into one pot. It's a lot of fun to make it. All the random ingredients simmering together create a symphony of flavors. Smoked chicken, Andouille, and crab claws. Soup bowls bursting with okra and sassafras and parsley flakes and cayenne amongst other peppers, and let's take a tour to Avery Island to see where they make Tabasco. We'll go down where the inlets of the Gulf begin trickling in. We'll go to a magic world where the Mississippi River meets the Gulf of Mexico. It's an incubating place exploding with life. Pelicans soar through the air like baby pterodactyls. The air is palpable; you can taste it on the back of your tongue. It's real. In a world of strip malls, asphalt jungles, and concrete towns, Louisiana is still real. It's a place where you can buy a snow cone for fifty cents from a kid fundraising for his Sunday school class. I sit back, take it all in and absolutely love me some Louisiana.

October 1990

Still hot as the blazes, and it's freaking October. Unbelievable, but things are supposed to cool down after this weekend. The sun just set. I'm at Dr. Landry's house, post inspection. He has a semi-neglected yard, but it's pretty charming, nonetheless. Dogwood trees and azalea bushes create an oasis in the heat of the day. There are some very nice hardwood floors throughout the house. The wood looks like Brazilian Koa. The house looks to be built in the '20s. It has tall, arching ceilings and wide, curved doorway arches. Stately crown molding provides character at every angle.

Many of the walls have built in bookshelves. The books form a labyrinth throughout the house and must exist to sate a Minotaur with an epic intellectual metabolism. It looks like the freaking Library of Congress in here. Along the hallways, black and white photographs line the corridors between bookshelves. All the photos are scenes of Louisiana. There are pictures of Huey and Earl Long, Lake Pontchartrain Bridge, St. Louis Cathedral, the Preservation Hall band, streetcars and anything else you can imagine that makes Louisiana unique.

Walking into his kitchen made me almost shriek with delight. He has a 1960's style art deco kitchen, complete with retro-inspired appliances. There is an old-fashioned icebox, blender, oven and dishwasher. The detail of the tiles on the counter and in the floor (as well as the backless swivel stools against the kitchen counter) effectively recreated the sentimentality of a soda shop. I sat at one of the stools for a while and wondered what it would be like to be with Dr. Landry, and to cook him breakfast in his wondrous kitchen. On the counter, he had left a container of koi goldfish food and a note of instructions for taking care of the house.

I figured I might was well check out the koi pond and feed Dr. Landry's fish. I went outside and immediately found myself in a circle of life situation. An enormous blue heron was walking alongside the koi pond, watching the fish swimming around. He was angling to make them into a meal. I threw open the screen and called to the heron. "Hey!" I yelled, hoping that was sufficient. The heron gave me a perfunctory glance and went back to monitoring the koi pond. Then he dunked his head in and began fishing. I ran towards the pond, which was at the back of the extensive yard. When I was about ten feet away, the heron whirled around to face me and his neck went all the way up. He must have been six feet tall when fully erect. His reptile eyes blinked at me, and he opened his wings wide to fly away. As he did, I yelled, "Stay away from the fish, do you hear me? Stay away from these fish!" I panted a little and watched him fly off. He was majestic and beautiful and all that, but Dr. Landry isn't paying me to have his koi depleted by waterfowl non grata. Most of the afternoon, I read books in a hammock by the pond to ensure the heron did not return for supper.

I'm sleeping in Dr. Landry's room tonight. He's got a big mahogany sleigh bed that looks like the cover of a home furnishings ad. The bed in the guest room has books on it piled three feet high and the living room couch is too short. He has no central air conditioning, just a window unit in his bedroom. He's also got a humidifier thing called a swamp cooler. Claude must not find out about swamp coolers, he would reference them for the rest of our lives. This swamp cooler in particular is cranked to the max—hope it cools off soon. I'm hovering in that place between sleep and awake, thinking about Dr. Landry. If I ever get up the courage to tell him how I feel, it could be an awfully big adventure.

October 1990

He came back EARLY! And what a disaster it was. About five o'clock this morning, I heard a noise and woke up. Dr. Landry was sitting at the foot of the bed—his bed—with me in it. I sat up fast and hit my head on the reading lamp—his reading lamp—I had been using. On his face was an odd blank look, as if seeing me for the very first time.

"You're here," I gasped. "Why are you here?"

"I *live* here." His eyes looked like the green flash of a sunset crashing into the horizon.

"You're back early. I must have fallen asleep." Like that explained this.

"So it would seem." No expression whatsoever. I couldn't tell if he was going to think this was hilarious or use it as the reason for my inevitable expulsion from Audubon College. There was no explaining why I was sleeping in his room, decked out in a sexy little nightgown, no less. It was white satin with red cherries, and he was looking at it. "Are those cherries on your nightgown?" He inquired, but he was clearly just looking for something to say.

My voice fought to conceal an imminent panic attack. "I thought you were coming back Monday. I couldn't fit on your couch and the guest room has like three hundred magazines on the bed. And I thought you were coming back *Monday*." My diary was sitting at the foot of the bed, not far from his knee. It was open, too. I tried not to have a conniption at the idea of his reading it. No—he wasn't like that. He was way too classy to read my diary.

"The conference wasn't all that interesting, so I decided to come home. Now, this—this is interesting." He waited to see how I would respond. I guess that's what they mean by sexual tension. "Well, I should go and let you get dressed." He again waited to see how I would respond. Was he calling me out? Was he trying to teach me a lesson? I was paralyzed with fear and completely speechless.

"Listen, Veronica," Dr. Landry finally said. "I can't help but think that at least part of you knew I could come home early. And you did choose to wear a very sexy nightgown. I would consider myself lucky to be with you. But it wouldn't be right, because you're a student. It's an abuse of your trust, my position, and ethics in general."

I felt like a complete idiot and sensed he might have delivered this speech before. Perhaps this kind of thing happened to

him all the time. He'd probably had at least a dozen glassy-eyed hero worshippers darken his doorstep over the years, right?
He sheepishly handed me a throw blanket, silently encouraging me to cover up a bit more. He said that this wasn't a big deal, and not to worry about it. He said that I would thank him later.

"I'd be open to revisiting this conversation when you graduate. If we're both single at that time, we could go out on a date or something. But that's three years from now. You'll find some guy your own age by then and forget about me completely." Dr. Landry laughed, trying to put me at ease.

"I'm just here because you asked me to house-sit for you. You're not even supposed to be here today." I breezily ran a hand through my hair to convey my indifference. He gave me a look that indicated he knew I was lying and started to get up. "Wait, please. All right." He waited to hear the rest. I took the deepest of breaths, as if going under water for an extended period of time. There was no turning back now. "Yes, you're right. I like you. I always have, and the thought of you coming home early had occurred to me. Didn't think it would actually happen, but I thought about it. And in my daydreams, I've hoped that aside from all the art stuff, you could also teach me . . . that." I hid my humiliated face in my hands, but could still see him somewhat. He was trying very hard not to smile, the bastard.

"Oh, Veronica. You are so sweet, and I'm beyond flattered. But my beautiful girl, I can't."

"Why not?" I asked. For some reason, the possibility that he might say no had not even occurred to me. Had I known it was going to go like this, I would have thrown the house key back in his face and run away screaming. This had quickly escalated into the most humiliating experience of my life.

He sat down again next to me. "Because it's not what I do. I feel it would be taking advantage of you, and that's not cool. Your parents are gone and your uncle hasn't really shown you much support." He held my hand. He had very nice hands, perfectly manicured and smooth as marble. Compared to other hands, they almost seemed like a reproach.

"You have such a nice way of putting things," I sighed in adoration. "It's so . . . southern." I had tears of shame and regret streaking down my face.

He handed me a few tissues. "Any decent person would do the same. You're emotionally fragile. Besides, why in the world would you want some old guy like me anyway?"

"I just wanted the first time to be special. With someone who wasn't a goofy high school kid or obnoxious frat boy."

He looked very surprised. "Your first time? No. It's not right. Save that for someone you love."

If you're going to make a fool out of yourself, might as well go all the way. "I already did," I told him. Where the courage came to even have this conversation remains a complete mystery.

His eyes misted slightly and his voice was as gentle as falling leaves. "You don't love me. It's just the romance of it. You're just looking for a father figure. I know the drill. Think about the reality of what it would mean if we were actually together. Dating. What are we going to do, walk hand in hand around campus with people gasping and pointing? We might as well have our reputations assassinated."

"Yours might improve. Anyway, we don't have to tell anyone."

"I'd love to—I just can't." He wasn't even pretending to entertain the idea.

As kind as the rejection was, it was still a rejection. Embarrassment burned hot in my cheeks. "I'm such an idiot," I groaned, burying my face in one of his pillows. "I should have never told you." The pillow smelled like him, a clean scent of talcum powder and cedar wood. It somehow made me feel even more pathetic.

Dr. Landry did his best to help get me past my shame. "You're not an idiot. Your feelings are valid and you are entitled to them."

"Other teachers date their students, you know," I told him, deflecting his rejection as if it wasn't a big deal. "There's a talk show about it every week,"

"Well, nevertheless, I'm not going to be one of them. Lots of people do lots of things. It doesn't make it right," he informed me softly. He was being so careful with my ego that he had to understand how much this hurt. "Veronica, please don't be upset about this. You should be out with guys your own age. You're young and beautiful. You're sweetness and light. And you are hard to walk away from, so please, give a guy a break, okay?" He quietly and graciously left the room—his room—and closed the door.

I looked in the mirror, silently judging myself. I had no idea who that was looking back, but she wasn't anyone I cared to know. I threw my clothes on and went into the kitchen. Dr. Landry was filling a bowl with cereal and milk. He put it in front of me and smiled warmly as though nothing had happened. I felt like I was four. After finishing the cereal, I packed up my bag to go back to the dorm. Dr. Landry was very polite as always. He thanked me and insisted on giving me the full $100.00 for watching his home, even though it wasn't for the full weekend. He said it was only fair, that a deal was a deal.

I was in the car when I opened the envelope with the money. There was a little card, too. It was an invitation to have crème brûlée at his house after I graduate from college. Yes, he read my diary all right. He was peeking out the window but vanished when my head shot up in recognition of the fact that he had read my innermost thoughts. The horror, the horror!

How am I supposed to face him now? I guess I should have thought about that earlier. You know you're a bad girl when you try to seduce your teacher, lie about it, and then get called out on the lying. I am now safe and sound in my dorm room, chastity intact. He's a good guy. I know that he'll never mention this to anyone else—maybe not even to me. He thinks I'm a stupid kid with a crush and maybe he's right. Thank goodness I had never made such a fool of myself with Dr. Jonas, my high school tutor. Claude might have shipped me off to an orphanage.

I had to shut the window just now. A cold front has arrived out of nowhere. Wicked weather this way comes and fall is finally here. It certainly feels like change is in the air.

4 THE AWAKENING

August 1991

Dr. Landry never acted weird about The House-Sitting Incident last year. At least one of us can behave normally. I still can barely look him in the eyes, so he finally came up with a solution. For the previous project, he had me stationed right outside his office. Now he's got me as far away from him as possible. He's banishing me for the time being. It feels like being banished from court, as though he is Louis XIV and the art department is Versailles. I've been excommunicated and ordered to assist the theatre department with their set design. The project is painting a series of murals for several weeks. Life will pretty much fluctuate between the theatre and Gumbeaux for a while.

September 1991

There's a boxing studio across the street from the Audubon College campus. I was passing by today en route to Gumbeaux. Through the window, I could see one of the boxing students working out. It was the bouncer from my art show, the 'ninja' who attacked Claude. He was slamming his bag with lightning speed and force. He turned and our eyes met through the glass. He cocked his head to one side as he tried to place me, and then it seemed to register. He threw me a manly sort of wave and I waved back. Then he went back to smashing his punching bag. Adrenaline was surging through my body so sharply that my scalp started tingling, and I ran the rest of the way to work.

November 1991

Had the strangest dream. Did not like it one bit. Just woke up and decided to try and capture it. There were two trains, running on the same long track. They were both running peacefully, silently, concurrently. But there was a sense of dread that something terrible and disruptive would happen, and it did. The two trains crashed directly into each other when they met on the track. There was smoke and fire and noise, screeching brakes and fear. It seemed to go on for hours; it seemed like it would never end. Like purgatory, like this would be reality forever. Then, as suddenly as it began, the trains made it through. All was peaceful and quiet again. All you could hear was the chug, chug, chug of the respective train engines. But underneath the peace was an uncomfortable certainty that another train wreck was inevitable. The only question was when.

Still not tired. Making some hot chocolate. I'm a hot chocolate fiend. Mom always used to make me hot chocolate when I had nightmares. But life throws you curve balls and then you have to make your own hot chocolate.

The nightmares have been severe lately and have inspired me to create a series of vivid, angry paintings. Granddad used to tell me to paint from the soul and out of love for the craft. He said that would be therapeutic and healing. What are the colors of the soul? I've used a lot of black and white and red. Fire engine red, that is. After a few paintings, I'm worn out and have to rest. Exhausted from feeling too much, feeling so raw. Going back to bed now.

November 1991

You aren't going to believe this. The good-looking boxer guy I saw at the local studio, the self-proclaimed ninja who slammed Claude against the wall? He just transferred to Audubon College from LSU. His name is Braden Davis. He's apparently a hotshot local actor, and he was just cast as the lead in *A Streetcar Named Desire.* He's going to play the brute, Stanley. Life at the theatre is about to get a lot more interesting. He came in today looking like a Greek god and wearing a T-shirt that read *No One Cares What Actors Think.* I was trying to paint a set and got so distracted that I nearly fell off my ladder.

I called George and asked him to tell me everything he knew about Braden. George disclosed that Braden held the undisputed title of Cool Guy #1, had women chasing him constantly and that anyone with any sense should look elsewhere for a love connection. George said that Braden was interested in martial arts, acting and seizing the day. It was the part about seizing the day that was the most problematic, as Braden was a card carrying hedonist. When I explained that I was already a little smitten with him, George advised me to run.

November 1991

There's a wonderful sense of camaraderie amongst the Audubon Players; that's what the acting troupe is called. They're joined by a love of theatre. They get the jokes when reading Shakespeare. They're fine with devoting entire weekends to set building and prop collection. Best of all, they've made me feel incredibly welcome. The love of the theatre is their only requirement for an invitation. You might be a coke fiend or incredibly religious or from another country, it doesn't matter. Their diverse talents result in a talented project team that puts on spectacular plays. Bayou Bend is too small to have a formal theatre group, so members of the community sometimes join the college's productions. It's the only lucrative department on campus; actually turning a profit due to charging admission (the students go for free, the public pays nominal fees). The Audubon Players' productions often sell out; they're very popular.

The theatre students know what's going on well before Mr. Fitzgerald makes announcements. The main campus teacher's lounge is directly below the costume department. Another student showed me how we could spy on the professors and eavesdrop on their conversations. Most of them weren't that interesting, but it was fun to watch the academics taking a shot at the title of Smartest Guy in the Room. One day, I was by myself sitting in there, and lo and behold, Dr. Landry and Mr. Fitzgerald appeared, shooting the breeze and snacking on Natchitoches meat pies.

"So, how is she?" Dr. Landry asked Mr. Fitzgerald.

"How's who?" responded Mr. Fitzgerald, looking around the room for artificial sweetener.

"You know who, Fitzy. Veronica."

"Just kidding, Dick. I know who you meant," laughed the director.

"Don't call me Dick," snapped Dr. Landry.

"Well, then, don't call me Fitzy. Besides, I've been calling you Dick for ten years, why would I stop now?" Fitzy playfully threw a stir stick at him.

Dr. Landry deflected the stir stick. "You never answered my question. How is she?"

"Veronica? She's great. She's doing really good work. She's got a lot of talent, as you must know, and she's here all the time." Fitzy looked like he was holding back information and was ready to crack.

"That's good." Dr. Landry seemed relieved.

"We'll see. Hey, guess who I just cast as Stanley for Streetcar?" Fitzy giggled like a schoolgirl.

"Who?" Dr. L was irritated that all he could find was non-dairy creamer. "I hate this powdered crap so much."

"*Braden Davis*," answered Mr. Fitzgerald triumphantly. He was really enjoying himself.

Dr. Landry had just taken a swig of coffee and spurted it all over the table. "Oh, no!"

"Oh, yes." Fitzy looked as though a viral plague had just swept through the room and got a rag to clean up the table.

"How did *that* happen?" Dr. Landry was pissed. You could hear it in his amazing voice. He should narrate audiobooks.

"What? I cast him because he was born to play the lead in *Streetcar*; he's perfect for it."

"I guess. Braden Davis? Really?" He looked a bit nauseous.

"Braden freaking Davis," concurred the director. "He's a natural star. Can't you just see the marquee?" He asked, spreading his arms wide, picturing its grandeur.

"Yeah, he's a star all right. There's no denying that. She doesn't have a prayer. Shame." He rubbed his forehead. "I saw him earlier today. He was wearing a T-shirt that said *I'm Not a Gynecologist, But I'll Take a Look*."

Mr. Fitzgerald burst into laughter, much to Dr. Landry's annoyance. "Are you sorry for sending her here?" Asked the director.

"Yes! Clearly this was a bad idea! She's a nice girl for Pete's sake. I didn't send her over here for Braden Davis to turn her out or something!"

"Didn't you send her here for that, Dick? Didn't you?" They were both quiet a long time. Fitzy sipped his tea (pinky out) from an elegant Victorian age teacup, while Dr. Landry drank from an NFL

Saints mug. They made quite a pair. "Hey, don't worry about it. You did the right thing."

"I don't know," said Dr. Landry. "She's so fragile and Braden Davis? He's a criminal! He could take her down a really bad path."

Fitzy swatted the comment away like a mosquito. "Nah! We live in the most gossipy city in the world. We would know immediately if he tried to do that. Besides, she just wants to start a new life, like you said. It is so tragic about her parents," he sighed, obviously empathetic to whatever the hell Dr. Landry had told him.

"I had to get a little space between us," Dr. Landry responded, ever the amateur psychologist. "She's crazy about me."

Fitzy rolled his eyes in disbelief. "Of course she is, Dick. Just look at you. Remember what Willie was telling that customer at Gumbeaux last week while we were having drinks? Don't get your honey where you get your money."

"Classic. Thanks for the tip." Dr. Landry sighed and began washing out his mug.

"Stop worrying about it. You did the right thing, Dick. She'll date Captain Fun and forget all about you." Fitzy grinned sadistically.

"Stop calling me Dick, Fitzy. And stop introducing good girls like Veronica to bad influences like Braden Davis. Good girls are already hunted to extinction as it is." They left the lounge, and I felt that the world had just gone from black and white to full color. Dr. Landry really did care, but I could not believe that he told Fitzy about my parents.

December 1991

Today Willie put up a sign that read, "There will be a $25.00 surcharge every time we have to hear about how much better things are in New York." Mee-yow! Someone must have said something about how much Tabasco he puts in the Bloody Marys.

I don't usually work the night shift, but Sue Bell the night supervisor needed a favor. She frequently needs a favor. Sue Bell tells customers sob stories about how her water heater is broken, or how her car needs new tires, and she ends up getting more tips. She's ridiculous. Lulu wouldn't be okay with that either. Bubba is not exactly minding the store to his wife's specifications.

Betty Boudreaux and I have gotten pretty close, being co-workers and all. She's quite wild and a lot of fun. Betty has lived here in Bayou Bend all her life, so she knows everyone. Betty and I were standing around trying to decide if we should get another case of Dixie beers from the cooler. We looked over to see Braden Davis come in. He was with two other guys who were similarly attractive. Betty exhaled loudly to convey her annoyance. "Do you see that guy with the black hair who just walked in? That's Braden Davis. I've known him for years. I went to high school with him. Braden was 'invited to leave LSU'—his words, not mine —for excessive partying. I hate him," she hissed.

This was disturbing news. I was hoping Betty would help me catch him. "He's playing Stanley Kowalski in *A Streetcar Named Desire*. He's over at the theatre with me every day, so I already know who he is. So what happened? What did he do to you?"

"What did Braden do to me? Nothing!" She threw up her arms in bewilderment, like he had to be out of his mind. "That's the problem. He blew me off, that's what he did! I was in love with him and told him so, and he wasn't interested! He says he's not into blondes. What's that all about? And besides, my hair isn't blonde—it's golden." Betty was fuming.

So blondes need not apply, huh? Nice. Braden had seen us and was walking over, a little stiffly, as though he'd hurt his ankle. He was wearing a T-shirt that read, *Tell Your Mom I Said Thanks.*

"Hi, Betty. Is this goddess actually your friend?" He was looking at me when he said it. My face had to be as red as boiled crawfish.

"Hi, Braden." Betty was very polite, like she had no issue with him whatsoever. I'm learning that Southern women are fairly complex. She introduced me to Braden.

"She's working on *Streetcar* with me, Miss March." He was talking to Betty but staring at me. I was starting to tingle.

"Shut up. How did you hurt your ankle?" Betty wanted to know.

"I was helping a little old lady cross the road. All of a sudden, she stole my wallet and kicked my ass. It was probably your grandmother." Braden had a very sincere, grave expression as he told us this. I tried to determine what celebrity he resembled most.

He could have been the love child of Robert Downey Jr. and Mickey Rourke, both circa 1985.

"You're the only thug around here, Braden. I'll bet a million dollars you were fighting again."

"Keep your *Playboy* money. Maybe I was fighting again, but you should see the other guys. And you should have seen me in action. I was amazing. Veronica, you would have wanted me *so much* if you had been there." What a disarming smile. His teeth were perfect. If you look up 'mojo' in the dictionary, there might be a picture of this frigging guy.

"It seems like someone would have been able to kill you by now," sneered Betty.

"Many have tried, none have succeeded. They're just a bunch of amateurs, sitting around wishing that they could be me. Cheap imposters everywhere." Braden grinned at me. "I'm sure you're much nicer than Betty, aren't you, Veronica?"

"Yeah," I grinned back and then saw Betty's face. "I mean no. Our niceness is pretty comparable."

"Am I making you nervous?" Braden asked in a stage whisper, moving in a little closer.

"Well, I have seen you hit. It's a little intimidating." I laughed nervously.

"People can only intimidate you if you let them," he told me, "and everyone has a weakness."

"Including you?" I asked.

"Of course," he concurred.

"Like what?"

He stared at me for a moment, laughed quietly and walked back towards his friends. Betty was really steamed.

"Everyone has a weakness," sneered Betty, mimicking him. "See how awful he is? I hate him. I mean, I truly hate that man. He's just flirting with you to make me mad. The only weakness Braden Davis has is Braden Davis. He's got a temper, that one. He'll be in a good place, and then his dark half shows up and things get all messy. What a waste."

It was hard to concentrate on anything besides the way Braden filled out a T-shirt. Where are the Calvin Klein talent scouts, why aren't they all over this one? "Betty, would you be mad at me if

I went out with someone here in town you used to like or date? Like Braden, for example?"

Betty laughed. "I've been out with everyone in town anyways, so I don't get to be mad about that kind of stuff. I'm going to have to start dating people in New Orleans because I've already dated everyone in Bayou Bend. Besides, this is a small town and terribly incestuous. It's impossible not to have some overlap." She proved her sincerity via her warmest, blondest smile.

"For real? I don't want to step on your toes," I told her.

"Yes. For real. Besides, you'll never land that one, not in a million years. Happy hunting." She clinked my glass with hers, giggling adorably.

December 1991

It's the middle of the night. I just woke up after having the weirdest dream. George was Peter Pan. He came into the nursery, and I of course was Wendy. My pseudo brothers, fake John and fake Michael, were asleep. George was saying in a stage whisper, "Come away with me, Wendy. Come away, come away!" He wanted me to fly off with him to Never Never Land, leaving my normal person life behind. We were off in pursuit of pirates, Indians and Lost Boys. It was chilly with the window open. I could see my brothers shivering in their beds, still asleep.

All of a sudden, George turned into Braden. And then he wasn't just Peter Pan, he was Puck. He was Huckleberry Finn. He was Superman. He could take me to galaxies even further away than Louisiana. Looking at Braden, it was impossible to miss how much life was inside of him. How he couldn't wait to go have fun, to dive into the next possibility, to chase windmills, to do it all. To do whatever. Who am I to refuse the call to adventure? I flew away with him to Never Never Land, selfishly not bothering to wake up my quasi-brothers for the fantastic voyage. When we got there, who was waiting for us? Claude, dressed up as Captain Hook. The strangest dream, really. The oddest dream. Going back to bed now.

Another dream. I had to get up and make a cup of hot chocolate because this one really got to me. In this one, I was seven years old. I was with my Dad, Enrique Fait, and my Grandfather, Jean-Luc; the coolest men who ever walked the planet. We were about to go cook steaks in the backyard. I was so excited. Then

Granddad handed me a flint rock and said I was going to need to build the fire myself or we'd never have dinner. At one point he used to teach survival skills while in the military. But I wasn't in the military; I was a little girl in a white gingham dress with red piping. I started to cry a little bit, and he and Dad sat down next to me. They were both so tall that it took them a while to get all the way down to my level. Dad said, "Granddad is right, Mary. You don't want to have to rely on anyone else. You need to be able to do this stuff for yourself because you may not always have someone else to do it for you." Then they showed me how to build a fire from tinder, kindling and sticks. It was so much fun. We were able to eat our steaks before the sun went all the way down and disappeared behind dense trees.

From this dream I woke up with my face warm and wet from tears. It was beautiful to remember them so vividly. There are still men of kindness and integrity out in the world. They're just hard to find, like any other priceless commodity.

December 1991

Lulu asked me to paint the Gumbeaux logo on the outside of the building. The logo is an alligator dancing with a crawfish. I said sure and spent most of the week working on it instead of waiting tables. It's done now and people like how it turned out.

We shot a commercial for Gumbeaux this week. The camera crew took tons of footage of the waitresses, New Orleans, our food, even the logo I had painted on the side of the building. Bubba made Clarence dress up like a big crawfish and dance around in front of the entrance. Bubba also tried to get Willie the oyster shucker to put on an alligator costume, but Willie told Bubba that he wasn't his n-word. Bubba got really scared and started apologizing like crazy. It was hard not to laugh. For background music, Bubba wants to use the song "*Hot Hot Hot*" by The Cure. The commercial would feature all the waitresses with shots of New Orleans and Gumbeaux. I asked if we needed permission from The Cure to use their song but he just waved me off.

Bubba himself dressed up in a smoking jacket, a la Hugh Hefner (you know that was Betty's idea). We had Kandace doing her fire spinning, too. I have no idea how she doesn't catch her hair on fire. She tried to teach me but all I did was bonk myself in the head. I didn't even try to light them. Also in the video, there's a scene where

Betty and I are dancing on the bar in our little outfits, and Willie sets the bar on fire. Hopefully we'll get copies!

Willie told me today that I seem to be searching for something, and he asked what it was. I said I was trying to find myself. He rolled his eyes and said that dumb rich white kids like me always talked about finding themselves and that we weren't worth finding anyways. I asked where he got the idea that I was rich. He said he always could tell when someone was "from money" and trying to pretend that they weren't. I protested but he just made that "Mmmm hmmm" noise. You know the one. So since he was still waiting for a response, he got the truth. If you find yourself, that means you get a new start. A do-over. And you don't have to be the person you are currently. You can just reinvent yourself. If Madonna can do it quarterly, the rest of us should get to do so at least once. He accepted that response and then brought me the best peanut butter pie you have ever had in your life. It was as if heaven commissioned Reese's to make Jesus' wedding cake or something.

January 1992

Betty had to squeeze past Willie in the hallway and accidentally rubbed up against his huge stomach. He then proceeded to tell everyone that he was tired of all the sexual harassment he received on a regular basis and was considering filing suit against us all. Catherine's response, "Willie, you trippin'!" spoke for all of us.

Willie, Catherine and I had a long talk tonight. I was telling them how I wanted to somehow decorate people's lives, to bring more color into them. To somehow make a facet of their lives better, even if just a little bit. That was the power of art, to ornament people's lives.

"So, you'd be like parsley, then?" asked Willie, taking a toothpick out of his mouth long enough to clown me. "You'd be decorating their lives like we decorate their plates, is that right? You basically looking to be a big old bucket of kale and parsley, then, is that what you're saying?"

Catherine was trying not to laugh. Apparently I had sounded a tad dramatic. "That's a very pretty sentiment, Miss Parsley. Maybe you can decorate my life and Willie's life by finishing up your side work, so the restaurant looks good for morning." Then they both laughed their asses off as I slunk away. It's worse than having a Greek chorus, believe you me.

Tonight I did my own side work of cutting lemon wedges and refilling ketchup bottles. Yuck. Usually I pay Clarence the busboy to help me out. Clarence and I shoot the breeze when the restaurant is quiet, like around 2 p.m. Once he pulled up his shirtsleeve and I saw a brand on his arm. His arm had BRG in large letters branded into it. My eyes got huge and I asked what had happened. He said it had to do with a gang he was in. I asked what it was called, and he said BRG stood for Brentwood Road Gang. Then he got really anxious and said he could be killed just for telling me that. I tried to be respectful, but what kind of sadistic gang brands its own members like cattle? And why would Clarence allow something like that to happen to him? So I said, "I guess the need to belong is stronger for some than others."

And you know what he did? He looked me straight in the eyes and replied, "I guess there are more options for some than others." Just because people in Louisiana speak slowly, it doesn't mean they think slowly. I wasn't about to ask Clarence to do my side work after that.

January 1992

The director/costume designer, Mr. Fitzgerald, is a real character. He is always sitting in the back of the theatre pretending to be an audience member who isn't enjoying the play. This is somehow supposed to motivate the actors.

"Why did I pay to see this?" he recently groaned in the middle of a scene. "Why didn't I just stay home, watch HBO and order from Pizza Hut? It would have been way better than this crap. Come on, people; entertain me! You're boring! That costume is supposed to have a scarf. Where is it? Go back to the dressing room and put on the costume as it was designed—now."

Fitzy is very finicky, but he does manage to get some stellar performances out of the actors. While rehearsing one scene that had a dog in it, he felt compelled to announce to everyone, "Look at the dog. He's the only one who's behaving naturally. He's in the moment and knows what he's about. No one else on stage knows. No one else apparently cares enough to deliver a realistic performance, only the dog. The dog is good. But the rest of you? Not so much."

I've been sitting in the audience at night, watching the play develop. It's fascinating to watch the process. So many people are involved in a play. There are people in charge of props, lighting, sound, scene changes, wardrobe, makeup, choreography. Each play is a project in itself. Some of the actors here are incredible; they could hold their own performing at the Kennedy Center. A few of the girls have caught my attention. Each of them is gorgeous, and at some point was involved in local beauty pageants. Each one has an individual talent (Irish dancing, baton twirling, what have you). They've been very kind and inclusive to me, even suggesting I audition for a part in the next show.

Some people have star quality. Some people have star power. I don't have those things but am comfortable with facilitating. Perhaps the whole idea of having a servant's heart is that you take joy from the happiness of others. So I may not be a big wheel or even a cog. But I am the grease in the engine that keeps it moving, on course. It's not sexy. Being the star is sexy. Not everyone can be the star. Some of us have to stand on the sidewalk and cheer as the star goes by. A star like . . . well, like Braden Davis. Now there's a star worth wishing on.

January 1992

The local boxing studio ordered sandwiches from Gumbeaux today. It was the end of my shift, so I intercepted the order and delivered it myself, hoping to run into Braden. He was there, wearing a T-shirt with a picture of Bruce Lee and the caption, *They Call Me Bruce*. He came over to say hi. He said I looked cute in my uniform and asked if the guy from the art show still gave me a hard time. I said that he was my uncle, and yes, he did. He asked if I would like to learn how to defend myself. I said yes, I would. He asked if he could show me a few things, and of course the answer was yes, he could.

Braden went to a storage bin, brought me a pair of cream-colored boxing gloves and wrapped ace bandages around my wrists. He said the off-white color was so everyone could identify the novice boxers. The intermediate students wore red and the advanced students wore black. Then he handed me a jump rope. He said the boxing classes began with five minutes of jumping rope as a warm up. What a nightmare, trying to get back to jump rope mentality. The rope was way too long so he was trying to help me by tying knots next to the handles. It was embarrassing to require a jump rope consultant. Then he helped me get into the boxing gloves. "It's nice that you're interested in learning. You came to the right teacher."

"For boxing?" My eyelashes fluttered, full-on coquette. I was well aware that flirting with him was flirting danger, like wandering mean streets and looking for trouble.

"Of course, for boxing. What else?" His eyes suggested that he knew what else—and how. He walked over and checked to make sure my gloves were on tightly enough. "Look at you in your training gloves. We'll have you out of those in no time. Want me to work you out a bit?"

"Sure."

"Have you ever tried boxing before?"

"Never."

"That means I get to mold you the way I want, and you'll be mine." He had me do fifty punches into a bag and held the bag as I did them. He made me go down a flight of stairs and jump back up, one stair at a time. After I finished jumping the stairs, he made me go back down and jump them two at a time. Then three at a time. After that it was, "Let's see you do thirty pushups, little girl. Drop and give me thirty." Then he made me do fifty sit-ups, and it went on like that for about an hour. I have never sweated so much in my life—he totally broke me down. I was like a boneless cat. He threw a towel at me and said to come back on Wednesday at 6 p.m.

Later that night, I was with Betty. She had received some flowers from one of our customers a week prior; and the flowers were starting to wilt. She removed the petals and placed them in a large glass vase. There were many layers of flower petals in the vase, already dried. She said they were the petals from all the flower arrangements she had received throughout her life, from people ranging from her parents to friends to male admirers. I asked why she was saving them.

"Well," Betty replied, "I'm saving them for my wedding. I am going to have the flower girl use these petals during my wedding ceremony. The petals from all these old bouquets will be laid out over the carpet. And then, I'm going to walk over my past and into the future." She smiled a very genuine, peaceful smile that I hadn't seen her use before. "That seems, you know—literary or whatever."

"Wow. That's pretty cool, Betty," I responded, shaking my head in admiration. "You're deeper than I thought, girl."

"I know. Keep it down, darlin'." She laughed and carefully placed the glass vase back in its location on top of the dresser.

February 1992

There's a directing class taught at the theatre department. In it, students learn how to direct a scene in a play. The student directors pick what scene they want to direct, cast it, costume it, et al. One of the acting majors in the class asked me to be in the scene she would be directing. I was supposed to kiss a boy in the scene, so I made up an excuse and turned her down.

I have like no experience with guys at all. I was home schooled before any of that really got rolling. Well, okay, I did have a brief thing with one boy a couple of years ago who was working for us as a docent. He smelled like overcooked cauliflower. I did kiss him on several occasions, though, just for the practice. It was either practice on him or on watermelons. Claude busted us. He was fired and I woke up to find that Claude had installed a lock on the outside of my room, so he could keep me from engaging in any more shenanigans.

February 1992

A Streetcar Named Desire has been a runaway hit. We have sold out every night and have a waiting list to boot. The reviews have been fantastic overall, but more than anything, the critics are madly in love with Braden Davis. When he screams Stella's name from under her window, it feels like the floor is shaking. His voice is that powerful.

Our cast party was held at Jean Lafitte's Blacksmith Shop in the French Quarter. Jean Lafitte's is one of the few remaining original French architectural structures in the French Quarter. It's located at the corner of Bourbon Street and St. Phillip Street. It was built sometime before 1772, and you can almost see the ghosts hanging around that place.

During the cast party, Mr. Fitzgerald had ordered Sazeracs for us and was in teaching mode about said drinks. He was really on a roll, too. "This is an absolutely exquisite cocktail—the Sazerac," he told us. "It's the taste of New Orleans and America's first cocktail, developed in the 1800s. Rye effused with spice and honey, bitters balanced with the sweetness, anise underneath and lemon oil dance inside your mouth. Savor it. Since absinthe is legal in the United States again, use that if at all possible for the sake of authenticity. Now, absinthe is a controversial drink. Who can tell me why?" asked the director.

"Because it was banned in the United States and most of Europe for its alleged hallucinogenic properties. That's why," deadpanned a familiar voice. I looked over to my right, and guess who was sitting just a few feet away? Braden Davis in all his glory. He was wearing a T-shirt that read *Leprechauns Are After My Stash*. My scalp started tingling at the sight of him. His eyes were locked onto mine, it felt like a tractor beam was pulling me in. "Hi, Veronica," he said, taking the seat next to me.

"Hi, Braden."

"Hi, Veronica," he said again, feigning coyness. "I've been meaning to ask you a question. Where are you from? I can't make out your accent."

"I don't have an accent; you have an accent," I replied.

"Only from where you're sitting, and we've got you outnumbered, darlin'." He grinned.

"Good point. It's a matter of perspective, isn't it? I'm from D.C., actually," I told him.

"What're you doing so far from home?" Braden wanted to know.

"This is home now. I wanted to start a new life, and New Orleans always seemed very exciting." He smelled amazing, like cedar and talcum powder and clean masculinity.

"You came here to find some excitement. Well, well." Braden seemed to find that rather amusing. "So, who's been your excitement tour guide since you got to town?" He ran his hands through his hair. He had thick, glossy, black, Italian looking hair. I could practically see myself in it.

I was getting distracted and tried to focus. "My tour guides? Oh, let's see. I have some friends at Audubon who have been really nice about showing me around, like George Graves. Betty Boudreaux as well."

"What? Veronica, no. Those people suck. You don't want them—you want me. I'm a hot young dude. I know about fun. They don't know about fun. I'll show you excitement. I'll show you a good time. But to be honest, I don't think you're ready." He laughed at my offended expression. "You strike me as a nice, sheltered girl and that's kind of rare. My Louisiana isn't all sugar and spice and everything nice—it's got a dark side. You'll need an adventurous spirit if you want to experience all that New Orleans has to offer. This is the most interesting city in America. It will get into your soul. It happens to newcomers. Here in this place, we've got something they just can't leave alone." There was magic, passion and excitement behind those eyes. Never Never Land lay behind those eyes. Those eyes belonged to a gypsy pirate who belonged to no one.

He stood up and held his hand out for me to take. His hand looked like he could crush bottles with it. I thought about Claude's hands. Claude has the hands of a wealthy man who does no manual labor. Claude says you can tell a great deal about a person by looking at their hands. Braden's hands were the hands of no gentleman, but you can't make an omelet without breaking some eggs. I gently pressed my hand into his and let him lead me outside, into the streets of the French Quarter.

Braden proved to be wonderful company and a knowledgeable guide. First, we went to St. Louis Cathedral. He lit a candle and said he was "Catholic, kind of." We sat in the incredibly beautiful historic church in one of the pews and looked at the stained glass windows. There was some kind of rehearsal going on, but we just blended in for a while and watched.

Next, we went to a four hundred–year-old perfume store where the staff creates scents for their clientele. They actually mix the fragrances in the store, creating a unique concoction for each patron. Braden told the saleslady that I would need something floral, soft and clean. The saleslady was a sexy brunette, dark and clad in black. She had long strands of glass beads bound by hemp about her neck and wrists. She was one of those girls who want you to think they're actually a vampire and just working a job so as to appear normal. Like they're Clark Kent or something. These girls are in D.C. too, part of the Anne Rice craze. Everybody wants to be a vampire all of a sudden. This particular specimen didn't have her canine teeth filed down to make them like fangs, but she had the rest of the uniform going on. Black vampy lipstick and nails, eggplant eye shadow, a tattoo that said "Transylvania Native," et cetera. She kept getting in my personal space. I got the impression that she was interested in a ménage à trois and that Braden was watching the scene unfold to watch my reaction. I pretended to be oblivious. Resigned, the Vampire Wannabe combined magnolia oils and lemon tree blossoms, creating a potion in her olfactory caldron. Once she had created my signature scent, Braden paid her and we went back out into the night. Caveat emptor indeed.

Next we went to see wonderful local artist galleries, like the ones belonging to Michaelopolos and Rodrigue. We went to Café du Monde for beignets. They were amazing, covered in heaps of powdered sugar so deep that you could practically do snow angels in them. We sat on the bank of the Mississippi River and just watched it moving, churning. All kinds of cargo went through the Port of New Orleans, one of the largest in the country. We talked about all the artists and writers who had celebrated the Mississippi River (and New Orleans) over the years. You could almost see rip currents along the huge serpent of a river. It's one of the world's greatest rivers. Africa has the Nile; we have the Mississippi. There was a huge log floating down the river as we watched. It gave some scale and perspective to the size and power of the river. The log was being swished about like it was a feather floating in the breeze, completely swept away by the current. The water's surface was fairly smooth, but it was clear that force and power had accrued in its depths.

At that point it was four in the morning. Uncle Claude always says that no good comes from being out at four in the morning. "It's really late," I said.

"No, it's really *early*," Braden corrected me.

"We should head back."

"Head back to what?" He wanted to know. "Come on. Let's get a room in the Quarter. We can go to the Richilieu or the Monteleone or something."

"I should probably get back to the dorm," I hedged.

"Why? Do you think that the Resident Assistant is going to tell on you for not coming back on time?" He laughed menacingly. "Because I'd smash his head in."

"No—because I'm not in the habit of staying with men in hotels."

"Given, but I'm in no shape to drive. Are you?" Braden asked.

I looked at the empty hurricane glass in my hand from Pat O'Brien's. "No. Probably not."

"A cab to Audubon College would be as much as a hotel here in New Orleans." He, like the rest of his kinsmen, pronounced it Nawlins. Watching me squirm and tremble, he gently touched the back of my neck. His charisma was palpable. It was hot enough to thaw my inhibitions. "Nothing will happen that you don't want to happen," he assured me quietly. "I promise." I nodded in acceptance.

There were loud noises across the Mississippi River, near Algiers. Braden said they were gunshots, and maybe we should get going. We went to the first little inn we could find, very cute. It was a bed and breakfast cottage. They only had one room available and it had a king size bed. It was a really nice room. He went to get us a bucket of ice. I paced nervously between cowardice and desire. When he came back, he had a bottle of champagne stuck in the ice bucket. "They didn't have champagne flutes. We'll have to settle for Dixie cups." He popped open the bottle and did the pouring. He sat down on the bed and gestured for me to sit next to him, so I did. He leaned over to kiss me, and then stopped. "Veronica, you're shaking. Are you afraid of me?"

"Yes," I whispered. "I guess I am." He considered that for a moment and looked around the room. His eyes fell on a couple of silk rope tassels which pulled the curtains back. He went and got them. I was really scared until he sat down and handed them to me. "What do you want me to do with these?" I asked.

Braden lay against the headboard and pulled his wrists back. "Tie me to the bedpost."

My head almost exploded at that one. "Um... what?"

"You heard me. Tie me to the bedpost." It seemed like a strange thing to do but very interesting. After I complied with his request, he was all smiles. "Now, are you afraid of me?" he asked.

"No. Can you really not get out of those?" I asked.

Braden tugged at his bonds. "Nope. Can't you see how utterly defenseless I am? You'll have to help me out with the champagne now." His blue eyes were like cathedral stained-glass windows, and I could almost see the light of his being pouring through them.

A strange peace came over me. I poured him champagne and helped him drink it. Then I leaned over and kissed him gently. Then, less gently. He let me drive, I was the one in control and it was dizzying. I unbuttoned his shirt to reveal his amazing body. I traced the edges of his muscles with my fingertips as he closed his eyes and breathed with pleasure. He had found a way for me not to be scared, and it was wonderful.

He kept his word. Nothing happened that I didn't want to happen.

March 1992

The Gumbeaux commercial is a HIT!!! They've been playing it locally. It was awesome to turn on TV and see it playing. Our sales have almost doubled since we started running it. We've had a line out the door all week. Bubba is in heaven, and so is everyone else. Even Lulu is stoked about the crazy good business we're doing all of a sudden.

I almost ran into Dr. Landry today. He waved and started walking towards me from across the cafeteria. I had no desire to see him and hid behind the salad bar. Dr. Landry probably feels like I've served my excommunication well and can return to court, but maybe I won't go back. I'm only supposed to be helping with painting sets, but Mr. Fitzgerald has me doing all kinds of stuff for him.

Being in the theatre and painting sets is so much fun that I don't mind, and besides, Braden is there. Tonight, Fitzy told me to help him change the colored filters for the stage lights. I followed him up a long ladder to the catwalks. They were up really high. Then, when I got close enough to the lights, he handed me this thing that looked like a bungee harness. He said we would both sit in harnesses, and slide back and forth, changing out the filters. The filters looked like stained glass but were made out of sheer colored plastic. I was scared to get in the harness but had to once Fitzy asked if I was "chicken." Once I was in, it wasn't so bad. It looked like we were rappelling off a cliff. Fitzy reached out to me. "Give me that one in your right hand."

"What color is this supposed to be?"

"Bastard Amber," replied the director.

"Bastard Amber? Who comes up with these colors?" I asked.

"I don't know, but some gig, huh? You should be good at this, being an artist," encouraged Mr. F. I am quite stellar at anything that involves color. Last semester, Dr. Landry gave me a color assessment. I had to arrange about twenty-five little color capsules in order of color, and the variation was incredibly slight. Lavender to medium lavender and twenty-five shades in between. I received a color score of "Superior." Dr. Landry said that people saw color differently throughout the day, that one's color senses were generally sharper in the mornings. He taught an entire class called "The Psychology of Color," which I loved.

"Did you ever notice that fast food restaurants usually use a lot of red and yellow in their advertising and branding?" Dr. Landry had asked us in class. "It's because those are hot, exciting colors. Red is a particularly exciting color, and that's why fast food restaurants use it in their branding and marketing efforts. Red makes you excited, and red makes you hungry."

"What about a woman wearing a red dress?" asked a male student.

"Like I said, red makes you hungry." A few of the guys in class chuckled. "Marketers use color to elicit response," Dr. Landry continued. "People are programmed to respond to color. Pantones are colors that are actually patented and have a number. This is to ensure that the color is exactly the same hue, no matter where it's generated." He went on to discuss how we associate baby boys with light blue and baby girls with light pink. The colors used for traffic lights, uniforms, government vehicles, direct mail advertising—all are carefully chosen to elicit responses.

Dr. Landry ended the class with a little-known true story about the French painter Henri Matisse, after whom I had named my cat. Matisse walked into a café and when all the patrons stood up to applaud him, he turned to his friend and said, "They must think I'm Picasso." Dr. Landry told us the point of the story was to believe in ourselves and not to sell short our abilities. It could happen if we wished it. We applauded him and believed in ourselves and he was the reason why we did.

April 1992

Haven't written in a while. Have gotten into whirlwind romance with Braden, which has escalated dramatically. He unlocked a serious passion from deep inside of me, which came as quite a surprise to both of us. He makes me feel like the most seductive and gorgeous creature in the world. He just stormed over me. What a force of nature. How could I have struck gold on the first try like this? He's thrilling to be around. He gives me goose bumps at the slightest touch. His smell is intoxicating. His skin is addictive. The unbridled energy of someone that powerful—he could crush me like an egg if he wanted to, but he doesn't want to.

I went over to his house recently. He opened the door holding a gun and wearing a T-shirt that said *See Me About Free Spankings.* "Do you always answer the door with a gun?" I asked.

"No. Not always." We walked into his living room. Braden must have had thirty guns lying around on the floor, several of them dismantled. He absently scratched his armpit with the gun handle. "I was just cleaning them."

"Yes. It looks very sanitary," was my sarcastic response.

A few of the guns looked pretty hardcore. It was like walking into a documentary about suburban gang warfare, or even a scene in *Goodfellas.*

"Are you allowed to have all this?" I asked, imagining some form of law enforcement busting down the door.

"Do I strike you as someone who cares about that sort of thing?" Annoyance permeated his tone. "I wouldn't be restricted by the rules anyway. Read the Constitution sometime, Veronica. We have a right in this country to bear arms!" He shook his fist at the universe for emphasis. "I've been collecting as many as possible for a while now."

"I collect stuff with turtles on it," I offered.

Braden ignored that. "I got my first gun—of my own, I mean—when I turned eight. My grandfather used to pay me for killing rats in the grain shed at his farm. He used to give me a quarter for every rat. I had enough to buy a car when I turned sixteen."

"Wow! You were shooting rats for money in the grain shed when you were eight years old? No judgment, though, and no judgment about your grandfather's judgment."

"Someone's got to do it," he said shrugging his shoulders. "What do you want, rat crap in your food?"

"No!" I answered, feeling nauseous at the very idea.

"See? I was providing a valuable service. The food of Louisiana is famous throughout the world. No rats were going to crap in it on my watch."

"It's too bad the USDA couldn't be here tonight. A shame, really." I was trying not to snicker.

"Are you making fun of me?" He seemed shocked that anyone would dare to do so.

I grinned inwardly and sat down between two rows of guns. "It's funny to see all these guns here. Dante gave me a gun so I'd fit in. I thought he was just exaggerating."

"Who's Dante?" Braden wanted to know, looking around for a particular type of ammunition.

"My lawyer." At this moment, it dawned on me that most college students might not have lawyers.

"Your lawyer? Why do you have a lawyer?" Braden looked puzzled. He probably could use one, thug that he was.

"Oh, um... you know, he's a friend of the family," I hedged. Good thing Willie wasn't around for this conversation, he'd never let me live it down.

"Good to have a lawyer for a friend, I guess. I could use a few lawyers as my friends. So, have you ever shot a gun?" He wanted to know. I told him that no, I hadn't. "I'll teach you," he said. "We'll go to the gun range in the morning."

Later that night, we went swimming. He took me to a very elegant gated community and we parked at the clubhouse. It was well after pool hours, and Braden proceeded to scale a nine-foot chain length fence in order to get inside. I balked and he asked why I have to be so boring all the time. I practically sprained my ankle on the way down. He advised me not to go into cat burglary at any point in time.

Swimming in the sparkling pool at midnight was well worth the misdemeanor. We lay on a raft and I told him about all the constellations, and the stories ancient peoples had crafted about them to better understand their world. He rubbed my feet and explained the principles of reflexology, and that each section of the foot correlated to another part of the body. He massaged between my toes until I thought I might lose my mind, then, as if knowing I was close to release, he backed it off, gently putting me back on the ground as easily as he had lifted me up.

May1992

Braden and I went back to the gun range today. Each time we go, the guns keep getting bigger and bigger. Today's seemed like a hand cannon. I was able to hit today's targets reasonably well, although my fingers are still a little numb.

Before we left, Braden started chatting with another customer in the lobby. He was an older gentleman and named Earl. Their conversation was about a third party named Satchmo, who turned out to be Earl's dog. Braden was trying to tell Earl that he wanted to give Satchmo a good home in his old age, and asked how much he wanted for him. Earl said he still needed Satchmo to guard his business, but that Braden could be his godfather. Braden acted as if he had just won an Oscar.

"Who else besides you could handle him?" Earl inquired. "You're the only one he seems to like."

"He didn't like me when he gave me this," declared Braden, pointing out an angry looking scar across his Achilles heel.

"You had it coming," Earl reminded him in a jovial tone. Braden agreed that yes, he did in fact have it coming.

"What did you have coming?" I wanted to know on the way back to the car.

Braden had a faraway look in his eyes. "Oh. Well, you know, Veronica, I used to be something of a punk..."

"Used to be?" My tone was more incredulous than intended.

Braden ignored the slight and continued his story. At age sixteen; he had gotten in a car accident, which bent the doorframe on the driver's side. Since he was low on funds and his father had told him to fend for himself, Braden decided to just steal a door from another car. He broke into a local car junkyard called Cypress Auto Parts and located the car door he needed. As he was attempting to pry it off, he heard a snarling noise behind him, and turned to meet a ferocious dog. Even in the dark, Braden could see the dog's eyes glowing like coals in the darkness. He tore off as fast as he could with the dog's razor like fangs snapping at his legs. He said he had never been so terrified in his life. He leapt for the fence and made it, but not before the dog sunk his teeth into Braden's heel. He did escape, but not without requiring about fifteen stitches and two months on crutches.

"My father was furious with me." Braden winced a bit at the memory. "He made me work for Earl. I earned the money to pay for the car door that I needed. And during that time, I got to know Satchmo, and he decided that I was okay."

I asked where he got the name Satchmo, and Braden told me that was Louis Armstrong's nickname. He expressed his surprise at my not knowing that and said that if he were as ignorant as I was, he wouldn't let on. "Satchmo is a crooner, and that's why he got his name in the first place. When the moon is full, or when fire trucks go buy, he howls. It almost sounds like he's singing – hence the name."

All that talk about Satchmo must have prompted a social call, because fifteen minutes later we were walking into the Cypress Auto Parts junkyard. Braden waved at an old man making coffee in a dirty little shack of an office and told him we were going to visit Satchmo. The old man just shook his head like we were out of our minds and then disappeared behind an endless row of cars. We walked up and down the property. Braden produced what he said was a dog whistle. I bit my lip to keep from laughing. Before this, I had no idea he was such a dog nerd.

"So, I guess it's safe for me to be here?" I wanted to know, although it was a little late to be asking.

Braden paused to look at a 1967 Ford Mustang that had been pulverized and was nearly unrecognizable. "Oh, no," he said, distracted by the rims of the car. "It's not safe, not at all. Satchmo is technically a Belgian Malinois, but he's more like a wolf. He's pretty feral. He insists on sleeping in a hole in the ground that he dug himself, although he has a bed and a doghouse."

Night had begun to fall. The old man he had greeted earlier lit a few citronella torches around the perimeter of the property to ward off bugs and darkness. A low rumbling sound began coming from under a car. I started to gasp and Braden clapped a hand over my mouth.

"I'm not kidding, Veronica. Stay where you are," he hissed. "No sudden moves. Don't you move, don't you freaking move." Then his eyes left mine, and he adopted a much softer tone. "Satchmo, it's Braden. Come one out, buddy," he called.

I did a double take because of the voice he was using. It was full of reverence and adoration. It was so unlike Braden.
I felt eyes on me from behind and whirled around to come face to face with an enormous black and brown wolf of a dog. I screamed and leapt into Braden's arms.

The dog circled around the two of us, still snarling. "I'm sorry, Satchmo," Braden whispered gently, as if addressing a toddler. "Veronica didn't mean to scare you." He put his hand out towards the dog, and it walked by close enough so that Braden could graze him with his fingertips. "That's how I pet him. You can't manhandle a dog like this."

"Is he going to kill us?" I whimpered.

He made a disgusted noise. "He's not going to kill *me*. He would have done so a long time ago if he wanted to. The jury is out on you, though. No more sudden moves," he warned. Satchmo sat next to Braden and poked his nose into Braden's pants pocket. He produced some bacon scraps, much to Satchmo's delight. "I try to come see him at least once a week."

We spent a while with the dog, and it really was something of a thrill to watch the way he and Braden interacted. He was like a wild animal handler. At one point, I got a little too close to the dog's face. I thought we were on good terms, but not good enough, because he flashed his teeth at me. I gasped and lurched backwards. "Dogs are like people," Braden quietly explained, distracting Satchmo with a piece of rawhide filled with peanut butter. "They don't like it when strangers get into their personal space." I agreed to make good use of that policy ongoing. We finally left the junkyard, and I felt I'd had all the excitement I could stand for one day.

May 1992

They have changed around some of the wait staff duties at Gumbeaux and it sucks to be me. Lulu said I have to mop the bathrooms before the shift starts, to make sure they smell extra fresh. Like they were ever extra fresh to begin with. Last week Sue Bell was in the ladies' room eating an oyster po-boy with the door locked. Customers were knocking on the door and asking her if everything was okay. I don't know why we can't just put extra air fresheners in the bathrooms. I have never had to mop a floor in my life. It's total bull crap. She can just get in there and mop her own stupid floor. She also wants me to scrub the sink with bleach. The fumes make me gag and Clarence is enjoying my pain entirely too much.

Betty told me that I could do a little better with my attitude. She caught me in a bad mood and I told her to screw herself, so she went to the walk in fridge, got a spray can of whipped cream and sprayed it into my face. I got a can too, and then things got a little out of hand. We were yelling at each other, and laughing at that point. Lulu came out of her office and was livid. She said we only had thirty minutes before we opened and that we were on thin ice. She made us mop the floor and bar area, and even Willie's oyster station. Willie came in while we were at it and was totally delighted.

"This is all your fault, by the way," Betty let me know with a giggle. "All I said was that you could have a better attitude about things. I mean, it is your choice to work here. You could go get a job in an office if you think you're too good to do side work and a little cleaning once in a while."

"I don't think I'm too good for it," I snapped, wondering if I would ever get the smell of oysters out of my hair.

Both Willie and Betty started laughing, and it was clear they had already had a conversation about my disposition. Maybe they are right, but either way, I had a hard time putting on a happy face for the lunch crowd.

June 1992

Braden took me to his family's house recently. When we entered the kitchen, there was an elderly black lady sitting at the table. She was listening intently to a HAM radio. The program was basically about not taking any crap from white people. She smiled at us when we walked in and turned down the radio (slightly). Later Braden informed me that she was their housekeeper, Florence. She had been with them since Braden was a baby and worked for them three days a week. She made us a couple of mint juleps. They had fresh mint and a sugar rim and everything. Here in Louisiana, cocktails are taken rather seriously. Florence asked Braden if he would please take a package of toilet paper upstairs with him and put it in the guest bathroom. "That's sweet of you to help her out. She's pretty old," I observed.

"Helping her? Don't let her fool you. She's in better shape than both of us. She just won't go upstairs." He looked as though he couldn't believe he had just said that aloud and looked down at his T-shirt, which read *Medicine is the Best Medicine*.

"Why not?"

"Um . . . just because of something that happened a long time ago," he seemed to be choosing his words with great care.

There was a photo in the hall of a guy who looked like the fishing guide that had taken George and me on our deep-sea fishing trip. "Is that your brother?" I asked. Braden nodded. "Is he here? Can I meet him?"

"No, Huey's not here. He's very rarely ever here. He has a place on the water in Venice (Louisiana, that is) and spends all his time there. He's a fishing guide who travels the state. He competes in tournaments, is sponsored by Bass Pro Shops, that kind of thing." Braden seemed completely disinterested in his brother.

I told Braden that his brother had been the guide who took George and me out during our Venice fishing trip. In the middle of my story, a young redheaded woman appeared in the bathroom doorway. "Hello, Braden. I didn't know you were here." She had a serious southern drawl, was wearing what looked to be a slip and was nursing a large plastic tumbler full of white zinfandel and ice.

"Hi, Candy," he said to her a little rudely. He introduced her as "Dad's girlfriend." We chatted for a few moments and went to a patio at the back of the house to nurse our mint juleps.

"Candy isn't your mom?"

"No, Candy is not my mom. No one's mom is named Candy; Candy is a stripper's name." Braden clearly had no respect for Candy.

"Wow! Is she a really stripper?" I wanted to know. I have an insatiable curiosity about strippers and prostitutes, not ever having met one.

"In my estimation: yes. I don't have any conclusive evidence to support my theory, though."

"Then, where is your mom?" I asked.

"We'll get along much better if you don't ask about that." Braden was trying not to go to the Dark Side but was hovering near it. He seemed a little tipsy and irritated, possibly because thinking about his deceased mom had made him defensive (just a wild guess).

He drummed his fingers on the side of his glass, staring at me. "It's the strangest thing. You give me the impression that you're trying really hard to blend in. Like you want people to think you're from here or something, but you're not. Why is that?"

"I'm trying to start over with a new life, so I'm embracing this one. It's just like I was telling Dr. Landry . . . " I was explaining, but then Braden cut me off.

"It's just like I was telling Dr. Landry," he said, mimicking me. "Richard Landry, huh? Don't tell me you've got a crush on him too. You and every other dumb girl at Audubon."

I was emboldened by the alcohol and said, "I'll bet you a million dollars that I'm smarter than you, Braden."

He shocked me by putting me in an instant headlock for several seconds. "If you're going to talk a bunch of noise, then you should learn how to fight. Otherwise, you'll end up getting your ass kicked all the time."

"Fine," I conceded. "We're both equally smart."

"It wouldn't be smart for you to fall for your teacher. It's very easy to fall for your teachers in life. Aside from our parents, they pay the most attention to us. What's not to like? But maintain perspective about what you're here to get."

"Which is?" I inquired.

"An education. Okay?" Braden squeezed my hand and looked very earnest. "Besides, he's ethical and everybody knows it. I'm not just saying this to be jealous, but you need to leave that man alone."

"Why?"

"Because being a teacher is a big deal. As a teacher, you're in an important position. You're shaping a mind. That's a responsibility and a privilege. It's like being a parent or guardian or caretaker. The students are following you as a leader. It may just be for a semester so they can pass the class, but whatever. They're counting on you to help them get a good grade, and to teach them something worthwhile. So keep that in mind and try not to screw it up for yourself." He could be pretty articulate when he felt like it.

I put on the Jane's Addiction song "Jane Says" (his favorite) and started doing a sexy dance for him. "You're wrong about Candy. She's not a stripper. If she was, I'd probably know her," I told him, tossing my shirt into his lap.

"Uh oh—she's seducing me again," sighed Braden happily.

Braden is something of a mystery. He's pretty shrewd and world-wise, for such a young guy. He's fearless and funny and so charming that he commands all the female attention in every room. And for the moment, he's all mine.

June 1992

Braden and I have spent a ton of time walking in New Orleans. The city is an ongoing, moveable feast. Today, after going to Mother's for oyster po-boys, we went to the edge of the Mississippi River and watched the Natchez Riverboat go by. It was full of laughter and light and people having a great time. They were dancing to the strains of jazz music; it looked like a wedding reception from what people were wearing. What a spirit and what a place. Braden is very patriotic about Louisiana. He hasn't had much occasion to travel yet, but looks forward to seeing the rest of the world after college. We discussed plans to tramp across it together. We thought we would go to Mexico first, then South America. Then Europe. Then Africa. He wants to avoid Russia because some girl he used to date lives there now. That's fine. We'll go to Istanbul instead.

We had a pancake making contest today at work. I came in second! I made three different buttermilk pancakes in a stack. One was blueberry, one was chocolate chip and one was banana. I called it the Bayou Bend Pancake Trifecta. Catherine (of course) won; she made these delicate little pecan pancakes that were so good they brought tears to your eyes. They dissolved into sweetness on your tongue, like crepes. She taught me how to make crepes last month and how to stuff them with Nutella. All the waitresses keep getting into the Nutella and it makes Lulu mad.

Another interesting thing happened last week. Several of the Audubon professors were having a meeting outside on the veranda. The Dean of Students asked me to get him some remoulade sauce. I went to go find some, but we were out. Dr. Landry walked by the register and said hi. I told him we were out of remoulade.

"We're going to want some for the fried oysters. Can you make some more?" asked the professor.

"I don't know what's in it," I shrugged.

Clarence was standing nearby. "It's got Dijon mustard, mayo, ketchup, lemon juice, horseradish, paprika and cayenne in it," Clarence informed us. He took out the ingredients from the walk-in fridge and set them on the counter.

"I still don't know how to make it, though," I told Clarence and Dr. Landry. "I don't know what the ratios are."

"Well, do you know what color it is?" Dr. Landry inquired. "All you have to do is get the right shade by putting them together."

I looked down at the colors. They did kind of look like paints, sitting there in front of me. I started mixing them together, using a plate as my palette. In no time I had figured out the correct quantities for remoulade. Dr. Landry tried it on a cracker and nodded. "That's awesome. You nailed it! Nice work. Hey, don't look now, but you just *blended colors*." He was right, I had. I looked up in surprise to see him smile graciously and mouth the words, "You're welcome" before casually strolling back outside to join the rest of his party.

June 1992

Took the trash out tonight. There was my crow, on top of the dumpster. He hadn't been there the last two times, so I thought he had moved on. I was dragging this huge bag of trash behind me. It was really heavy. I should have asked for help but didn't want to trouble anyone. The crow flew down and landed on my trash bag. He started pecking at it. He started trying to break open the bag to get at what was inside it. I tried to shoo him away but he wouldn't leave. I looked up and Clarence was watching me through the window. He had the strangest look on his face. Then when I turned my attention back to the crow, it was gone. Clarence came out. I said, "Did you see the size of that crow?"

He looked quizzically at me. "There was no crow. That's twice now. You crazy. You best keep your waitress money, girl, cause you're gonna need it to pay a head shrinker one of these days." It's so weird that he missed it. How did he miss it?

Braden and I went out tonight with another couple. His T-shirt du jour had a gingerbread man on it and read *Totally Baked.* We went to a Japanese steakhouse, his favorite. He always tries to bond with the chefs as they cook table side. He feels they're kindred spirits because of his interest in martial arts. They always look semi-annoyed when he does it, which is hilarious. At one point, he went under the table and starting kissing the inside of my leg. He's wonderful. I look at Braden and know that there will always be a little piece of my soul with his name on it.

On the way out of the restaurant, we ran into one of Braden's many discarded women in the lobby. Her name was Shelia. Braden's eyes got as big as saucers when she came out of the ladies' room and saw Braden. She walked over to us. She wanted to know why Braden never called her. He said that he had been busy. Shelia wanted to know who I was. She was really pissed. She glared at me. I thought she was going to attack me at first, but then she hauled off and hit Braden in the stomach before storming away. He was not expecting it and it actually hurt him a little. I told him that you have to pay to play. He told me he could never be serious about Shelia, since she was really a blonde who just colored her hair black to impress him. "I didn't even want to go out with her in the first place, but she kept calling and showing up at my place," he complained. "What was I supposed to do?"

"You can't be bringing your emotional B.S. into the pimp game! You cracker-ass cracker!" I bellowed in perfect imitation of Willie the oyster shucker. Braden loves that kind of stuff and started laughing hysterically, so his stomach hurt even more. Serves him right, unscrupulous cad that he is.

After dinner we went to one of the riverboat casinos in New Orleans. Boy, are they fun! There's no thrill like winning. My favorite is roulette. I'm really good, I have my own system. I put chips on every number on the board. I keep winning although Braden said I'm a moron and my dumb luck will run out sooner or later. I was holding some of Braden's money that he was up. He said he was a compulsive gambler and to please keep the money for him so he didn't spend it. I was wearing a pair of shorts and put the chips in my pocket. I didn't know there was a hole in the pocket. As I walked by the blackjack tables, I'll bet people were diving for the floor as I unknowingly left a trail behind me, not unlike Hansel and Gretel. It wasn't until Braden asked for his money that I reached into my pocket and felt nothing but the hole.

He thought I was messing around when I said it fell out of my pocket. He went through my purse. At one point he found a garter in there, grinned, remembered he was angry with me and kept looking. Finally he believed me and we left, him storming through the casino with me in tow. "You know I'll take it out of your ass," he assured me. I had not seen anyone get that angry except for . . . well, except for Uncle Claude, actually.

June 1992

Braden and I saw a great movie tonight, *The Silence of the Lambs*. It was an amazing story about a psychologist who is jailed for cannibalizing his patients, but then helps the FBI catch a serial killer. Braden keeps pretending to be Hannibal Lecter, the main character played by Anthony Hopkins. He keeps pretending to be Hannibal and he always wants me to recite Jodie Foster's movie lines.

In other news, Willie and Clarence were planning to run a body disposal service out of Gumbeaux today. They didn't know Betty and I could hear them talking. They were talking about how local mobsters could drop off people they had murdered, and we would cook these individuals. Willie and Clarence would incorporate their remains into our crawfish etouffée and smoked brisket sandwiches. No one would ever be the wiser and they would make a fortune. You could just drop off anyone who had caused offense, and Willie and Clarence would make them vanish forever. They would be legends of the underworld. They're probably just talking a bunch of noise but nevertheless, I'm keeping an eye on those two.

June 1992

Where do you go when you disappear? Lately for me it's been Lake Beatrice. It's a beautiful lake about fifteen minutes away from Audubon College. I like to go there at times to just sit and look at the water. You can see waterfowl, turtles, fish, and snakes on a regular basis. I keep looking for the alligators but haven't seen any yet. I even tried to find them on one of those Louisiana swamp tours. It was a guided expedition in a glass bottom boat. It had just rained, the sediment was all haywire and you couldn't see anything. The swamps are so dark and mysterious. I keep thinking about the slaves and scofflaws who hid there, and of those who still do to this day. There aren't very many places to hide in the world anymore.

Everyone is getting cell phones and cars that ensure you never veer off the predetermined path. But I like the road less traveled. I just like the idea of getting lost in a place no one could ever find you.

Lake Beatrice's best views are at the Bayou Bend Boathouse. All the people who consider themselves Bayou Bend's elite go there on the weekends. There, they assess each other in terms of romantic eligibility and level of attractiveness. There are a lot of forty-something women squeezed into outfits from Bebe and Forever 21. They're on the hunt for sixty-somethings because the men in their age group are after twenty-somethings. Such a vicious cycle. I was able to go to the Bayou Bend Boathouse because Betty loaned me her family's membership number. She was going to meet me in a couple of hours, and then we would go out on her boat.

I had brought some art supplies with me and was drawing a picture of the lake. There weren't too many people around yet. I could see turtles sunning themselves on cypress stumps and fish jumping into the air. There are a few amazing houses around the water, but it's fairly undeveloped. I wondered what it would be like to have a house on the lake. I love the water and can stare at it for hours. The thing that fascinates me most about water is the way it changes color under the sun every moment. Subtle hue shifts that go on all day and night. It's a reflection of the sun and sky and air—a body of water is alive and changing constantly.

"Why hello, Miss Veronica." I'd know that voice anywhere, under any circumstance and spoken in any language. He sure gave James Earl Jones a run for his money. I looked up to see Dr. Landry, hair slicked back and eyes twinkling. "I haven't seen much of you around."

That was because I had been avoiding him, but it wasn't because I didn't enjoy being around him, I had just been terribly embarrassed about the house-sitting incident. "How are you?" I said, happy about this unexpected surprise.

"Very good, and better now." He pulled up a chair next to me. He put his coffee cup down next to him. "It's wonderful to see you. I didn't know you belonged here."

"Well, I don't know if I *belong* here, but I've got a guest pass. Do you have a boat here?"

"No, I have to rely on the kindness of other boaters. But I'm just happy to be out here next to the water. It's a peaceful place to paint, draw, read and think." He looked at my drawing, and he smiled as though he liked it. He had a newspaper with him and read it as I drew.   •

We sat next to each other in silence for an hour or so, doing our respective things and imbibing caffeine. I was basking in the sunshine and his presence. It just felt good to be around him. I wasn't embarrassed anymore about that incident at his house. Something about it felt like when you're a little kid sitting in the back of a car and your parents are driving. You knew they would take care of everything, and that you were safe.

Then something eclipsed the sun. I looked up to see Braden standing over us. He was there with a couple of friends, who hung about twenty feet back. He was staring right at Dr. Landry. He had assumed a semi-dominant posture. Today's T-shirt had a large shamrock on it and read *Rub Me For Luck*.

"Hi, Braden," I greeted him with an uneasy smile.

"Hey, Clarice," Braden said in his best Hannibal Lecter voice. He is fantastic with imitating all kinds of voices. Unfortunately, though, he's still hung up on *The Silence of the Lambs*. "Is this your uncle?"

"No, Braden. This is Dr. Richard Landry. He's a professor at Audubon College, and it seems like you'd know that, having lived here your whole life," I snapped.

"Oh. Didn't recognize you in the sunglasses. What's up, Dick?" Braden asked.

"I don't go by Dick, but you can call me Richard or Dr. Landry," said Dr. L evenly.

"Oh. Sorry. I was told that you prefer Dick." They were sizing each other up. Dr. Landry wasn't smiling. He was looking at Braden like he was a bug that needed to be squashed. Dr. Landry sure has some cojones. Braden was always looking for a fight, whether he was willing to admit it or not. He used a lacrosse stick to take out four meth heads last week. One of them dinged his car door, and he used it as an excuse to beat them all up. I didn't like it. I didn't like that he liked it. Real martial arts people don't pull that kind of crap (according a documentary he made me watch about Bruce Lee).

Ever the gentleman, Dr. Landry paused long enough to let Braden know he was not intimidated and then politely excused himself to get another cup of coffee.

Braden called menacingly after Dr. Landry, "You use Evian skin cream, and sometimes you wear L'Air Du Temps, but not today!" Dr. Landry ignored him and his *Silence of the Lambs* quote.

I smacked Braden with the newspaper. "Did you have to ask if he was my uncle *and* call him Dick *and* do your Hannibal Lecter impression? So uncool!"

"Sorry to interrupt. I thought I was saving you. Besides, what do you care? Do you like him or something?" Braden looked annoyed.

"Yes. I do like him. Very much, in fact. I like him a lot better than I like you, especially right now. He's worth at least five of you. Maybe more," I estimated.

"He is not."

"I'd need a calculator to know for sure. Besides, Dr. Landry has been really nice to me." Well, for the most part, at least.

"Of course he is." Braden shrugged. "You have everything he wants."

Statements like that are always a red flag for me. "Oh yeah? How so?" I wanted to know.

"You're a good artist. You make him look good. Aside from that, you're pretty hot," was Braden's response.

Relief washed over me. Braden still doesn't have a clue. There's an outside chance he might hold me for ransom, if he ever finds out my net worth. I wouldn't put it past the thug.

"It's not like that, and he doesn't think of me that way. He's my teacher. You know, like Obi Wan." I wondered what they charged for Kahlua with coffee, and if I had enough cash for the bar.

"Obi Wan? No. I don't think so. You got that same dumb, lovesick look on your face as the last time you mentioned him. Don't answer right now, but give it some thought. Are you looking for a father figure? Girls do that sometimes, you know," he told me.

"I like Dr. Landry a lot, so stop it. I am not listening to this." I started walking away.

He followed me, and his voice raised an octave. "Veronica, you're not supposed to fall in love with Obi Wan. You ask him to help you understand The Force and that's it. Leave that man to his good works and stop being a distraction. If you get involved with him, it won't end well—mark my words," warned Braden.

I was annoyed. "Things usually do end badly; otherwise, they wouldn't end. You don't get to have an opinion on this; it's none of your business. He doesn't want me. I already tried." It seemed like that might shut him up.

He looked appalled. "You tried? I sure didn't need to hear *that*. There's something about you I want to protect. I have kind of a weakness about you."

"Everyone has a weakness," said Betty, who had just walked up to us. She looked incredible in a tiny red bikini. "Hi, Braden. Do you and your little friends want to join us?"

How he was impervious to her charms was beyond me. "No. I do not want to join you." Braden replied coldly before giving me a disgusted look and rejoining his party. I was nervous and wondered if I should try and further communicate with him, but Betty pooh-poohed the idea. She was ready to get out on the lake, and frankly, so was I.

We took out an eighteen-foot Yamaha ski deck boat. Betty excelled in most sports and unsurprisingly was a terrific water skier. It was my job to drive the boat. About lunchtime, we were pretty hungry. From her cell phone, she ordered some food from a nearby waterfront restaurant. We drove the boat up to the dock and they actually brought the food out to us, complete with a twelve pack of beer. You should have seen Betty showing off. She would put a couple of beers in her lifejacket and actually chug them while she rode her slalom ski. We told each other stories. I told her how much I hated my uncle, and Betty said she would have him eliminated if I liked. She said it would be as easy as a phone call. Betty is such a good friend. We took a nap in the boat in the middle of Lake Beatrice and greeted people we knew (she knows everyone). This went on all day.

Around 6pm, I was getting tired of being on the lake, but not Betty. At sunset, she suggested we go into the bayous and look for gators. She was sure she could wrestle one, if given the opportunity. That was the beer talking. Time to turn the boat towards the pier and tie it back up. Betty said this was how she spent her weekends, and that I made an excellent First Mate.

July 1992

When Braden and I celebrated Independence Day, I wouldn't have guessed we'd end up liberating an urn from an old graveyard. It wasn't a typical graveyard. Not the kind with headstones. Certainly not uniform in nature like Arlington Cemetery, where my grandfather and parents are buried. Braden called it a City of the Dead. Many of the graves here in Bayou Bend are built above ground, since the town is technically below sea level. If you don't bury people above ground, the caskets rise up. The tombs look like above ground marble boxes. They house the bodies and caskets. Some of them are up to eye level or higher. It's eerie, because as you walk around, you can't always see what's around the corner. In the dark, it's the kind of thing that nightmares are made of.

As far as the urn went, Braden had been eyeing it for a while. He said he wanted it to use as a base for a coffee table and it would make a great conversation piece. He said he didn't think taking something from a cemetery is wrong if the people have been dead a really, really long time. In this case, the urn was on the grave of someone from 1851. Braden rationalized it to me by saying, "It's not like people are still visiting them." Sure, like he really knows. What a thug.

When we were finished at the graveyard, he wanted to go to yet another messed up place, an old abandoned orphanage. Braden may be crazy but he's never boring. He actually had miner headlights for us to wear and said they were his dad's. We parked the car and got out. The place was falling apart—and probably condemned.

We put on the miner hats and turned them on. They didn't work very well; they had this lame flickering glow. His hat was blinking on and off at first, so we had to adjust it. I told him they needed new batteries. He told me I needed new batteries. He's such a child. We walked around the house to see if any doors or windows were ajar. We found a window with all the glass broken out of it. We made our way through, although Braden cut his leg on the glass. He always looks a little beat up.

Through the dingy light of the headlamps, we could make out a huge ballroom. There was no furniture, just an old piano that had been smashed up with an axe. The axe was still in the middle of the collapsed piano, the way it would usually be stuck in a tree stump when not in use. That was weird but we kept going, wondering if we would find any homeless people living in there. We found a long room full of beds. Braden walked up to one of the beds; it had these straps on it that looked archaic and evil. We realized they had been used to restrain whoever was in the beds. At that point, I was over it, but he wanted more. He said that he'd take me to the edge and then over it. Then he wanted to have at it there in the hall and was denied. That place was disgusting.

Braden and I next found ourselves in a bathroom. There was a layer of dust on everything, including the mirror over the sinks. And then I saw it. Someone had written *"GET OUT"* in the dust, like they scrawled it there with their fingernails. We were terrified and hightailed it back to the Mystery Machine (Candy's powder blue VW Golf). If we keep this up I'm going to have a heart attack.

When we were pulling out of the haunted house, there were fireworks lighting up the night. They were incredible, reflected in the remaining water of the neglected swimming pool. They weren't as spectacular as the ones they do over the Washington Monument or anything, but pretty fabulous nonetheless. "Braden, there's something I should probably tell you," I mumbled quietly as we were driving away.

"What?" He looked amazing, even wearing a T-shirt with a picture of a piñata on it that said *I'd Hit That.*

"You were my first," I confessed. It seemed like he should know, for some reason. Might was well be tonight.

"Your first what?" It sunk in. "What? No. No. That couldn't be. No. I... would have known. Right? Wouldn't I?" He looked really traumatized.

"All right, you don't have to believe me," I muttered.

"Are you kidding me right now? Are you kidding me?"

"No, I'm not. It's the truth," I shrugged. Clearly it was a mistake to have said anything.

"You're lying; you have to be." His face was lit up in multicolor by the fireworks overhead.

"Wow. I'm really sorry I told you." Tears started to well up in my eyes.

"The more I think about it, the more it makes sense. Thanks, Veronica!" Braden yelled. "What the hell? Why are you telling me this now? Why didn't you tell me before?" He kept raising his voice because the pyrotechnics were coming to the grand finale, and they were pretty loud.

I gripped the door handle, just in case I needed to jump out of the car. "Because I thought you might not want to if you knew." This had really gone awry.

"You're right, I wouldn't have!!!" Braden agreed, raising his voice even more. "That's a lot of responsibility! You can't just spring something like that on a guy! That's something that should have been brought to my attention beforehand! Dammit! Girls! Unbelievable!" He was really hot under the collar. He drove me home (silent all the way), and then screeched off in Candy's powder blue VW Golf, leaving rubber marks on the street. The VW Golf isn't his car. It belongs to his Dad's girlfriend, Candy. It's hard to be a tough guy in a powder blue VW Golf.

When I got to my dorm room, I found a note on my pillow. Braden must have left it there before we left. I stretched out on the bed and read it.

```
To: The Beautiful Veronica Fey

At 5'o clock in the evening
On the day of independence
here in your dorm room
the windows are open
and the air is cool
and a picture of you
smiling, mouth open
pressed against me
is like a landscape,
the first slide in a zoetrope
whose circles spin outwards
and forward and down.

With a warm and happy heart and a hug.
-B.
```

It took a while for the magnitude of what I was reading to really sink in and take effect. Braden Davis writes…poetry? I reached for the phone to tell him how much I liked it, and realized that the timing was not appropriate. If he ever decides to speak to me again, we can cover it at that time. And who cares if he does? Screw that guy. I'm mad at him anyway, now that the hurt has subsided. Who acts like that when you open up to them? What kind of a reaction was that?

I decided George was a better person to call, so I got him on the phone and told him everything. He took me out to dinner at Commander's Palace to cheer me up. It's hard to have a lousy time at Commander's Palace. We had a blast and ate until we were four cornered. Wild rice shrimp remoulade, giant sea scallops, champagne poached crabmeat... I could go on for hours. For dessert we had Creole bread pudding soufflé, which they advertised as 'The Queen of Creole Desserts.' I closed my eyes to better savor and identify every individual ingredient. I expressed a little half-hearted concern about our caloric intake. George said these dishes were the stuff legends were made of, and I should just have fun and not even worry about the specifics.

George agreed that I should have told Braden. Well, no worries, he won't be calling anymore. I showed George the poem and he was so shocked that he started choking on his coffee. George said he had known Braden since grade school and could not recollect any of his women getting a poem. "And believe me, Veronica, there have been a lot of them," he assured me over his scotch julep. "At least a hundred, easy. Maybe two."

"Thanks, George, for that information," I responded dryly.

The gossip king still had information to divulge. "In 10th grade, his friends actually staged an intervention and told him it was going to fall off if he didn't slow down. And you're cute and all, Veronica, but he has had some really gorgeous women. One went to Chicago and became a model. One…"

"Thank you again for that information!" I shouted, angrily plunking two more sugar cubes into my coffee, trying to splash him in the process.

George batted his eyelashes like a Botticelli angel. "Looks like somebody's in love," he declared in a dreamy sort of way.

August 1992

I didn't hear from Braden for a few weeks, but he called me last Wednesday. He said he couldn't get me out of his head. He said he had a weakness about me that he didn't understand and wanted to know why I had chosen him to be my first.

"It was really more about timing than anything else," I assured him.

"Oh, thanks a lot, Veronica," he laughed.

"You're welcome," I purred back into the phone.

"Just me, huh?" His voice was softer than usual.

"Just you." I thought about visiting Victoria's Secret on the way over to his place.

"That must be why you're so bad at it," was his gentle response. He can say what he wants. He called me, I didn't call him.

August 1992

What an awful day. George wanted me to go with him to see his parents. He said his father wanted to "talk" to him and he said he needed moral support. It was pretty obvious that George's alternative lifestyle had come to his father's attention, and he was being called on the carpet. His mother was trying to make light of what promised to be an ominous, stressful situation. On the menu for tonight's confrontation and airing of grievances? Buttermilk fried chicken, cheddar cheese and rosemary drop biscuits, grilled corn on the cob, fried okra and Sock-It-to-Me cake.

When we got there, the lawn man was just leaving. George asked how it was going with the pair of peacocks that he had given his parents as pets. The lawn man said that the peacocks kept pecking at windows and scratching up the top of Mr. Graves's Suburban. He said that Mr. Graves shot the peacocks because of this. George was really shocked, then sad for a minute, angry for another minute, and then, worst of all, resigned. He took a moment to compose himself, and then we went in the house.

Mrs. Graves said I could help her set the table. I was folding napkins and putting ice in the glasses, but from the football-themed man cave, we heard trouble a-brewing. The voices started soft and slow but gained thunder levels and finally pitched screams. George's father was screaming that he knew what George had been up to, and what the hell was wrong with him? Where had they gone wrong in raising him? Didn't he understand that homosexuality was not acceptable in their family? It started to rain, and it was pouring so loud that I had to crane my neck to hear (without looking like it, obviously).

George was trying to be the peacemaker. You could tell even he had a problem with his own homosexuality. At one point he said, "Dad, think about how gorgeous Veronica is. Do you know how much easier my life would be if I could just be attracted to her? If I could just marry a girl and have kids? I know you won't accept me after this conversation. This family is my life; it's everything to me, and to know you won't allow me back in the house is devastating. But I can't live a lie, Dad. When Aunt Jean brought those medical journals over, way back when I was six years old, I remember going through them. I remember looking at the man, and thinking, that's interesting. I remember looking at the girl and not being interested at all. And there was no trauma. There was no anything of that nature. I just like men, Dad. That's it."

You could hear his Dad hollering and some items in the room getting broken. George's mother was a nervous wreck but kept slicing watermelon chunks. She put them in a big bowl and poured vodka all over them. "Do you really think that's a good idea right now?" I asked.

"Hey, you deal with your family drama your way, I'll deal with it mine," she snarled. I felt an inch tall. You can't say anything critical to people about their families. They aren't rational about it and will want to kill you. I've even caught myself defending Claude at times. Sure, he sucks, but he's all I've got.

George tore out of the den, grabbed my hand and pulled me out of the house. We jumped in his bright lemon yellow Mercedes coupe convertible (clearly his gay/straight lines had been blurring for a while). He drove away from his family's farm as if we were trying to get away from a fire. We didn't even go by to see his favorite horse or anything. He drove me to the bridge that he had thought of jumping off a long time ago, when he realized he was gay and there was really nothing he could do about it. The rain was coming down really hard, really nailing the little yellow car. There was a little tear in the rag top. I was trying to keep out the water with a T-shirt, but it wasn't working very well.

"This, too, will pass, George. Your dad has to deal with his life, and you have to deal with yours." I took his face in my hands. "Live your life, George. Live your life."

"I wish you could pick your family like you pick your friends," sighed George.

"Wishing is okay, but acceptance is better." We sat a long time looking the rising river, hoping the rain would stop and that the road wouldn't flood.

August 1992

Hot, hot, hot. It's the off-season. School hasn't started yet. Most of the students haven't returned and Gumbeaux is pretty quiet. I sat with Miss Catherine most of today in the kitchen. She was making gumbo. The first thing she did was take a penny out of her apron pocket, and she laid it on the stove next to a sauté pan.

"What's that for?" I wanted to know.

"That's for color comparison. First, you make a roux. See how I heat oil and fold flour into it, like making gravy? Then, you get it to the color of that penny. That's how you know when it's done."

We had learned about the origins of gumbo in Louisiana history class, and I started cataloguing a bunch of facts for her. Catherine got bored pretty quickly and told me that gumbo was more about action than words. She directed me to spend my energy on chopping up the holy trinity: onions, green peppers and celery.

She's taught me all kinds of cooking techniques. She taught me that if you take egg yolk and brush it on bread dough before baking it; it turns that fancy golden brown just like in Paris patisseries. She taught me that if you put a little vegetable oil on a spoon, then sticky substances like honey and molasses won't stick to it. She taught me that you can make your own buttermilk by adding white wine vinegar to regular milk. Hopefully someone is getting all of these tips down.

Catherine makes the best sweet potato pie in the world; that's what the customers say. She won't let anyone around when she finishes it off. She kicks everyone out of the kitchen and locks the door until she's done. It's some concoction of marshmallow topping, but no one can figure out how she gets this really nice crunch on the top. It's her little secret. I watch her bread the oysters and twice bake the potatoes. It's warm and pleasant hanging out in the kitchen with Miss Catherine. She likes me. Not all of the other kitchen employees like me, though. The line cooks definitely don't like me. It's because I busted one of them for stealing.

I answered a phone call from a customer last month. She said, "Could you please send your oyster boy over to my house again? I'd like to purchase another quart sized container."

We don't sell oysters by the quart or offer delivery service. "Ma'am, could you please let me know which one of our oyster boys came to your house last time?" I asked.

"Jerome," she replied.

"Jerome. Right. And how much was Jerome charging you for a bucket of oysters?" I inquired.

"Twenty-five dollars. Such a bargain, that's why I've got to get some more," the customer said enthusiastically as I cringed. Jerome was our night shift line cook. He was six foot six and could doubtlessly drop me like a bag of dirt. Apparently he was stealing (maybe he thought of it as liberating) tubs of oysters and selling them in local neighborhoods. The tubs were worth $54.95 each; that's what we paid for them through the seafood farmers' market. How long had this been going on?

When I told Lulu what had happened, Jerome was fired. Lulu then told everyone that I was the one who was responsible for Jerome's termination. The line cooks were pissed off and gave me a really hard time afterwards. They told the other waitresses that I was probably a white supremacist. When I asked for anything from the kitchen, they practically threw it at my head. I stopped requesting things like tomato slices and just let the customers deal with it. I don't have the stomach for all this. Hopefully this will blow over soon.

When I told Braden, he was completely unsympathetic. He said it was my own fault for being a snitch. He said I should have left it alone and maybe even covered up for Jerome. Then, the folks in the kitchen would have killed people on my behalf; they would have been so loyal. What kind of a response is that? Doing the right thing sure sucks sometimes, that's for sure.

The Kappa Theta Kappa fraternity is having a luau tonight at their frat house. Gumbeaux is cooking an entire pig for the event. They brined it yesterday and cooked it outside in this huge black smoker we have. It still has the ears and the hooves and everything. People either love it or hate it, no two ways about it.

September 1992

I got a really weird call from Claude last night. Braden and I were asleep in my dorm room. I just have a twin bed and he's a big guy, but for some reason, we fit together perfectly. Braden can sleep through a hurricane and didn't budge when the phone rang.

I picked it up and heard Claude mumbling something incoherent. There was a lot of noise in the background, and I could tell he was at a party. A couple of girls were giggling and asking him to get into the hot tub with them. He told them to shut up and then focused his attention back on our phone call. He was babbling a bunch of nonsense. "Everything happens for a reason. Even with everything that happened, and when I became your guardian. It really hasn't been so bad, right? I haven't been bad to you, have I? It's all been for the best. Hasn't it?"

It was as though he was begging for some kind of validation from me. Who does he think he is? Isn't it enough that he killed my parents? Now he has to try and get me to say that this, in retrospect, was preferential to having them alive?

Anger washed over me. "It turned out best for *you*. For you. Not for me, and not for them, but for you. Please do not call me in the middle of the night ever again." I slammed down the phone with everything I had, hoping his eardrum would explode.

My scathing retort woke up Braden. "Why are we awake?" He wanted to know, and then saw that I was very agitated. He suggested we go for a little drive, which was fine. There was no going back to sleep after that wake-up call.

Braden drove us to a duck pond near the college. I asked where the ducks were. His eyebrows rose anxiously, like he didn't want to be the one to tell me. With some coaxing, he finally agreed to do so, although he said he was reticent about divulging local secrets to outsiders. Braden then told this long story about a young boy who had gotten his hands on a few piranhas. The boy's mother ordered him to get rid of them, so he put them in the duck pond, which was just behind their house. As it turned out, the piranhas found the semi-tropical environment to be ideal and began to multiply exponentially. Braden said the ducks were smart enough to find another pond to inhabit. Even though the story was ludicrous, he was still very convincing (go figure, he's an actor). Just was I was starting to believe him, he picked me up and acted as if he were going to throw me into the pond. He had me laughing so hard that there was no more worry about Claude.

Then he took me out to a 24-hour diner and we had icebox pie (chocolate for me, and peach for him). Before we left, Braden had them wrap up a turkey leg for Satchmo. Braden said it was for Satchmo's birthday because he just loves watching him eat turkey legs. He says he crushes bones in his jaws as if they were potato chips. I don't care what people say about Braden, especially after seeing the way he is with Satchmo. Anyone who goes out of his way to take care of a friendless junkyard dog is a pretty good person in my book.

September 1992

Is Louisiana a feminine state or a masculine one? I guess she would be considered feminine, but not really effeminate. In many of the romance languages, the nouns are either masculine or feminine. The noun for cat is female and dog is male. The ocean is female, the earth is male. Venus and Mars. All words have a personality bent towards one or the other. Louisiana has so much duality. Just like the much coveted woman who's both the Madonna and the whore.

In the French Quarter, there are courtyards and little gardens in the center of some of the buildings, and they're open all the way to the sky. When I looked into this unusual and charming practice, I found out it was popular among the genteel women of the antebellum/Civil War period. It was so that the Rapunzeled ladies could have sunshine and fresh air. Their controlling husbands couldn't abide their women walking through New Orleans during that time period. Not unescorted. Ladies had to stay home and be in sewing circles and what have you. Only women of questionable character ventured out alone in the streets of New Orleans alone. Their husbands, wishing to protect their loved ones from the evil world, built them views to the sky so they still felt free. Gilded cages. New Orleans had been a dangerous place.

But why would anyone want to live in a boring place? What kind of a life is that? Artists don't live in boring places. Monet went to the jardins for a reason. Hemingway hung out in Key West, Cuba, Kenya, Paris et al. So did Granddad. Jean-Luc Fait was a great adventurer. He ran around the globe creating experiences. How are you supposed to be an artist if you haven't lived? What in the world would you have to create the art from?

September 1992

Betty and I did something a little crazy tonight. A lot crazy. We went to the house of this guy she's dating. We noticed there was another car in the driveway. You could tell right away that it was a girl's car because it had a lot of girly decorative crap in it. We could faintly make out some laughter, and I crept along the side of the house. We peered in the window. There he was with some girl. Right in the living room, with all the curtains open. Yikes. They were really going at it. You should have seen the look on Betty's face. She said, "Veronica, go to my car and get the gun out of the glove compartment."

"You have a gun in your glove compartment?!" Looking back, that was a question that didn't need to be yelled.

"A little louder, V, people in Texas won't be able to hear you!" Betty hissed. "Have you ever heard of the word 'stealth'?"

"Why do you have a gun in your glove compartment?" That was the only question on my mind.

"Who doesn't?" She asked in exasperation, stretching her perfect body to get a better look at her wayward boyfriend. "Just go get it!"

I was starting to wonder if he even really was her boyfriend. "No! I'm not going to Angola. This guy isn't worth it; don't do it. But if you do, you're on your own," I yelled at her. "If I won't go to jail over killing Claude, why would I go to jail for your stupid, pseudo ex-boyfriend? I don't even know his last name!" I yelled.

"It's Jacobson!" she yelled back, as though it made any difference. "I have to stay here and see what happens, please just go get it!" She screamed, getting a little hysterical.

"No. And I'm going to stop you from getting it, too." I assumed my perception of a karate pose. She was a danger to herself and no one else was around to help.

"Some friend you are," she hissed impatiently, looking around for other options. She spotted a hammer on the ground next to her foot. Thank goodness it wasn't a chainsaw.

Conjuring up images of a female Thor, Betty grabbed the hammer and heaved it as hard as she could through the window. The glass exploded, making a blood curdling smash, and the hammer landed in front of the couple. We could see their horrified expressions and hear their subsequent screams. The alarm systems went off and lights began to come on in houses up and down the street. We ran for the car. Betty drove us away from the scene of the crime like a bat out of hell. We made it down the road and hid in a park near the college. We looked at each other, both still panting and out of breath, and started laughing uncontrollably.

We spent the rest of the evening at the casinos playing blackjack, and ended up at a local greasy spoon around 2 a.m. The cook's hair had been shaved bald, except for a patch in the shape of a Fleur de Lis. When I pointed it out to Betty, she replied, "That's Peyton. He's worked here for fifteen years and gets his hair shaved to feature different shapes each month."

We consumed saltine crackers with Green Goddess salad dressing, red beans and rice with Andouille sausage, mustard greens with cornbread, icebox pie, and endless cups of coffee. About 3 a.m., we finally left, ready to crawl into bed for at least nine hours.

September 1992

Waiting tables has been quite an education. You can learn a lot about people from waiting on them in restaurants. You can learn a lot from a sociological perspective. There are the married men who stare at the waitresses like sex starved prison inmates. Then there are the little old women who gossip about all the other customers. There are the regulars who come in every day by themselves. There's the church crowd. There's the Friday happy hour crowd. There's the crowd waiting expectantly for us to open the door at 11 a.m., because apparently that's too late for some people. There are the people who want you to leave a pitcher of tea on the table at all times. There are the people who use all the sugar packets from their table, as well the sugar packets from the next nearest table. There are the lovers, the married couples, the fraternity boys and sorority girls, the local officials and the military personnel from the nearby Air

Force base (they come in wearing camouflage and we pretend we can't see them). There are parents who can't control their children and couples who like to get in arguments before a semi-captive audience.

What I'm realizing is that all people are basically the same. Most of them just seem to try and do the best they can with what they have. Maybe there are no bad people and no good people, either. There are only people with their own agendas, and people are basically okay with each other until their agendas intersect, creating an impasse.

September 1992

Sue Bell, the night shift supervisor, had a visitor today at Gumbeaux. It was her sister, Tammy. Tammy looked pregnant, which was odd, because she had to be at least fifty years old. I asked Betty what the deal was.

"Oh, that's her sister. You'd think she was pregnant. She looks pregnant. But she isn't." Betty is like a gossip oracle.

"What's wrong with her? Why does her stomach look like that?" I wanted to know.

"Take a closer look. It isn't only her stomach," hissed Betty in a stage whisper.

I walked by casually, trying to check out the swollen stomach in question. Betty was right. Her swelling went down into her legs as well. When I came back, Betty said, "Did you see?"

"Yes. What causes that?"

Betty looked at me like I was born yesterday. "Cirrhosis, darlin'." She then returned her focus to sorting the stack of dollar bills she had collected during her shift.

"Cirrhosis?" I repeated.

"Yeah, cirrhosis of the liver. Liver damage. She's an alcoholic. Even with her condition, she still continues to drink a lot. I'll bet a hundred dollars she'll get a drink here any moment, and it won't be Mountain Dew," she said knowingly.

I gasped. "You're kidding!"

"Wish I was. Her body can't process alcohol anymore. Or hardly any fluid, for that manner. She has to go to the hospital and get drained." Betty folded her stack of ones and tucked it into her bra. I'd never seen anyone do that before but decided to focus on the cirrhosis issue.

"They drain her? They drain those fluids right out of her body?" I asked, imagining that those fluids must smell incredibly bad upon extraction.

"Exactly," Betty agreed. "She has to go regularly and get drained. They juice her, just like an orange."

"Why doesn't she go right now?" I wondered, noticing how uncomfortable Tammy looked.

Betty hunted around the cash register for a pen with blue ink. She only likes to write orders in blue ink. "She can't go right now. She already tried calling the hospital. Her doctor's angry with her. He's been avoiding her calls. She knows she'll have to go to indigent care if she can't get him to do it, and she doesn't want to go there. This has been going on for years. It's nothing new." Betty was primping, using the mirror behind the bar to inspect her appearance.

"Why is he dodging her calls?" I asked Betty.

"He's probably fed up with Tammy's crap," Betty speculated. "She won't listen to him and continues drinking, although obviously she isn't supposed to. She's been drinking like a fish most of her life. If you were a doctor, and you gave people advice that they never followed, it would probably tick you off too."

"Sure it would. Betty? We're not alcoholics, are we?" I hadn't considered that before.

"Of course not,' scoffed Betty.

"How do you know?"

She paused, thinking about how to best respond. "Well, for one thing, alcoholics go to meetings. I hate meetings, don't you? Let's not go to any meetings."

Our conversation had become tiresome, so I looked across the bar, and there was Sue Bell putting a margarita into her sister's hand. My stomach hurt—or maybe it was my liver—just from watching this go down. Bubba came by and asked me if I wanted a drink. I shook my head and went in the back to hang out with Catherine.

Catherine was making Cajun stuffed potatoes. As soon as I appeared, she yelled for me to bring her more butter. I went to the cooler and got a huge five-pound slab of butter. Real butter, that is. She won't hear of using margarine, even when Bubba complains about the cost. I handed the butter to Catherine, who tossed the entire thing into her huge cooking pot. I was a little aghast, since I eat our stuffed potatoes pretty regularly. "How many calories are in one of those potatoes?"

Catherine looked disgusted. "Honey, do I look like I'm counting any calories? Child, please. Lord, have mercy! Now, do you want to learn how to make stuffed potatoes or not?"

So I learned how to make stuffed potatoes, and in the comforting warmth of Catherine and her kitchen, I tried to forget about Sue Bell's sister.

Catherine was really happy with how well I was learning, so she decided to reward me. "I'm going to show you how I do my secret pie topping. But if you tell anyone . . . " She pointed over at a voodoo doll she had sitting on a shelf. That was how she kept us all in line, threatening us with voodoo. I promised I wouldn't tell anyone (she didn't say anything about putting it in my diary). She shut the kitchen door so no one else could see.

We set up twenty-four sweet potato pie shells with filling (three rows of eight). She smashed medium sized marshmallows all over the tops of the pies, and then got out a blowtorch. My eyes had to be enormous, watching her light up a blowtorch and use it to sear all the marshmallows. "I always wondered how you got them done so fast," I gasped.

"Yeah, you knew I had a secret weapon. I've got things to do. This baby here, it's like having a magic wand."

"Can I try?" I was really excited to see if I could do it.

"Sure! Here you go." Catherine put it in my hands as if bestowing some kind of award.

I used the blowtorch and it was the perfect tool for singeing the marshmallows—almost like having a light sabre.

September 1992

It was an incredibly slow night at work because there's a fall festival going on downtown. The only people at Gumbeaux were Clarence, Bubba, Willie, Sue Bell, Sue Bell's sister Tammy, and Tammy's cirrhosis issue. Bubba let us all sit in the bar and have drinks. It was difficult for me to watch Tammy drink a pitcher of Whiskey Sours. When she had finished the last drop of her pitcher, she looked over and showed me all of her cards.

"I know what you're thinkin', darlin'," Tammy said. "I'm sure you're sitting there judging me." At this point, I protested but she wasn't buying it. "Hey, I was young and cute too, once. Let me tell you about myself, girl. I was born in 1955 and starting stripping about age seventeen. I met quite a few people at that job, and soon I was running with this local motorcycle gang called the Bone Crushers.

"They operated a roadhouse just outside of New Orleans. When I turned twenty-two, they told me I was too old to strip anymore. They said I would need to entertain the clientele in the back. Sometimes that meant different things, but it always involved substances for sale and the flesh trade. I didn't care. I did whatever they wanted me to do. It was all business. I was the best girl they had; they had me on this kind of long-term career path, they called it.

"When I turned twenty-six, they told me I was too old to service the customers in the back. I began tending bar. I tended bar and I watched what went on. They made me the screener to decide what customers got invited in the back. I was with their head guy. I was his lady. I did a real good job for them. I made them probably hundreds of thousands of dollars. Do you think I saw any of it? Do you think they set me up with a savings account? They did not. But I worked for them and was a loyal employee, nevertheless. So the head guy in charge, Nate, he took care of me most of the time, and we were together fifteen years. I was his woman, but one day I let him down real bad and things got ugly.

"One day, see, these three little bimbos came in the roadhouse. And they somehow knew we had fifty thousand dollars-worth of cocaine in the back room. I don't know how they knew, but they knew. They slipped something into my drink; they slipped me a ruffie or something. I passed out and they got a hold of Nate's cash box. Well, when he saw what had happened, he beat the crap out of me. Both my eyes were blacked out. My mouth was oozing blood everywhere. I was kind of still in a daze but could hear him talking. He was telling someone, "Take this stupid bitch out to the swamps and dump her there. She's alligator food, do you hear me? I don't care if she's my woman. Nobody takes fifty thousand dollars away from me and lives to tell about it."

"But thank God, he got really drunk and changed his mind, or I'd be dead for sure. When he realized how sorry I was, he said he'd let it go. He got killed about a week after that. Someone cut him in the gut and he refused to go to the hospital, so he bled to death. It's so hard watching the man you love die, girl. I kept saying, 'Nate, you have got to go to the doctor!' But he just told me to shut my hole. His face went from red to pink to white to gray... he just bled out. His life just was all over the floor, oozing out of him. If I could have put it back in there for him I would have. But I couldn't."

Tammy sighed and lit a cigarette. "I don't know why I'm running on and on. It's just that seeing you, you remind me so much of myself back then. I know you came here looking for an adventure. It's why I came here too. I'm from a little town in Arkansas you've probably never heard of. If I'm not a cautionary tale, then nobody is. What you see here before you is the result of a selfish kind of life. And ultimately, life is about choices." And then she took a long drag on her cigarette.

I came to college to get an education. I'm getting an education, all right.

September 1992

Bubba is in trouble. A lawyer called him on behalf of The Cure, and said that Gumbeaux didn't have permission to use their *"Hot Hot Hot"* song in our commercial. I knew he was being way too casual about it. Bubba sure has some brass, taking on Robert Smith of The Cure. Bubba acted like he didn't care, but we could hear him frantically canceling TV spots left and right through his office door. It was a shame because the commercial was fantastic. Bubba said he would just use a Jimmy Buffet song next time. Some people just don't get it.

Braden came into Gumbeaux to see me today. Betty told him I was in the walk-in refrigerator getting salad dressing. He had the audacity to sneak through the back door, found me and locked us both in the refrigerator. Whose boyfriend does that? Then he was on me like "white on rice," as Miss Catherine says. "Like a duck on a June bug." We broke a lot of health codes, I won't lie to you.

I've been working more hours at Gumbeaux lately. We've had a couple girls out sick and they've needed me to cover. My school work appears to be slipping, but who cares? Dr. Landry left a note that said, "See me" in my mailbox, but I'm not feeling it.

October 1992

    Betty and I worked at a beautiful catered event last night. It was about an hour away, in Vacherie, Louisiana (not far from Oak Alley). It was called Dauphine House. It was the most incredible Southern plantation home you can imagine (aside from Oak Alley). They wanted Cajun food and a couple of waitresses to serve it, so there we were. The evening was perfect. A hot day had cooled into twilight. There was a swimming pool with a black bottom, and little candles floated on the surface of the pool like sailboats. This was a special house, one on the National Historic Register that people paid money to visit. A running infomercial set up in the lobby declared that slaves were once maintained on the property. The narrator of the piece said it very quickly, glossing over the unpleasantness of that situation.

    I imagined what it must have been like to be the plantation owner. Then I wondered what it must have been like to be one of the slaves. This actual building saw stuff like that go down. History is crazy. I imagined the plantation owner seeing me working outside in the fields and taking a liking to me. All of a sudden I was ordered to be at his chambers at sundown. I imagined my fear and hesitation walking down the long hallway to his room, when the sun was but a green flash on the horizon. This was probably one of the better case scenarios amongst a small series of hideous options available to the enslaved.

    Betty whispered in my ear, beckoning me to follow her. We went around the back of the house to the pool area. The pool was enclosed with an eight-foot privacy fence. We could hear the clink of glasses, laughter, the bounce of a diving board and splashing water. Betty waved me over to a hole in the fence. Clearly she'd done this before. She looked inside, giggled and beckoned me to do the same, blonde siren that she is. I looked through the hole and couldn't believe it. It was a naked pool party. A bunch of the local elite, hanging out at a naked cocktail swim party. There had to be at least forty people in there. I wondered what Braden would say if he was here? He'd probably love it. Then Betty and I both got the giggles and ran off. We were supposed to be working, after all.

    Fireflies hung in the magical night air. The Dauphine House backed up to the Mississippi River, and we took a long walk alongside it before heading into the house. The management let us spend the night for free, since it was so late. Betty started playing with my hair. I asked if she was drunk, and she said yes, and leaned over and kissed me on the mouth. I've never kissed a girl before. She smelled like jasmine and tasted like strawberries. Braden doesn't know what he's missing.

Betty and I smoked a joint in the carriage house around midnight; some bartender had given it to her. Who knows what else he gave her, they disappeared for a while earlier in the evening. I had never smoked before and felt fantastic and float-y. I was sorry to know the house had afforded captivity for some, because I had never felt freer than I did on that night.

November 1992

George asked me over to his family's farm for Thanksgiving dinner, as he does every year. I asked if his father was around. George's father has a tendency to disappear for weeks at a time. You aren't supposed to mention it when he shows up again, as if he were some kind of runaway cat. You are supposed to act like everything is normal, as though he never left. George said it would just be the two of us plus his mom this year. He said it was going to be really mellow and we could just relax and have fun.

Late afternoon on Thanksgiving Day, we were having a great time at George's farm. We were drinking cinnamon schnapps and singing songs by a fire we'd built outside. Out of nowhere, Braden showed up. He was a little drunk, driving a beat-up Harley Davidson chopper, and wearing a T-shirt with a picture of Missouri under the caption, *Missouri Loves Company*. There was a sidecar attached on the left hand side, and Braden had a huge frozen turkey in the seat as his passenger. George asked him if he could ride around with him sometime in the sidecar. Braden told him yes, as long as George wore one of those helmets with a big spike on the top.

I asked Braden where he'd gotten the turkey. He said he'd liberated it out of his father's fridge because they'd gotten in a big fight. I imagined Braden running away with the turkey, not unlike the Grinch who stole Christmas. Braden brought the turkey in the kitchen and showed it to George's mother. She looked a little anxious because dinner was already cooked. Since she's a gracious southern lady, she didn't say a word, even when Braden hugged her suggestively. He just can't help himself. Once he was out of earshot, Mrs. Graves whispered, "My goodness, Veronica. Your young man looks just like a movie star." She's right. He really does.

George quietly asked if I had invited Braden over for dinner, and I assured him that I had not. Then Braden asked George for a deep fryer. It seemed improbable that someone would be able to set up a fryer large enough for a twenty-pound turkey with no notice. George likes Braden, so he shrugged and set one up outside within a few minutes. Apparently the Graves family likes to fry large items so frequently that it's a reasonable request. Once the oil was bubbling, Braden unwrapped the frozen turkey and prepared to drop it in the grease.

"You're not going to season it or anything?" I asked over his shoulder, wondering if this was the culinary equivalent of backseat driving. "You're just going to throw it in there?"

George hushed me and said to leave Braden alone; he was a grown man and could take care of himself. I wasn't so sure and ran to get a cookbook from Mrs. Graves. I found a page titled "Fried Turkey Safety" and was trying to read it to Braden:

Things to Remember When Deep Frying a Turkey

1. **Always use the fryer outside where there is good ventilation and solid ground; avoid using it on a wooden deck or near things that can easily catch on fire.**

2. **Thaw your turkey; any extra liquid could increase the chances of your fryer exploding.**

3. **Check the temperature of the oil consistently; some fryers do not come with a built it thermometer.**

4. **Protect your skin and eyes from possible oil splatter.**

5. **Make sure to follow the instructions for your deep fryer.**

Braden was literally doing everything the book suggested not to do. He wasn't accepting my feedback and said it was no big deal to drop a frozen turkey into a large caldron of boiling oil. We were right by the garage, so I got one of the heavy duty fishing poles George and I had used on our deep-sea fishing trip.

"At least lower it down with a line, Braden. This isn't our house, and we don't want to blow up anything."

Braden grabbed it and said to leave him to "man's work." He hooked the huge turkey, got on a ladder (the pole was ready to break) and lowered it into the oil. A huge fireball collected—it looked like a burgeoning mushroom cloud of flame. George grabbed my hand and pulled me out of the vicinity, right before it exploded everywhere. Flames consumed the turkey, the deep fryer and even the lawn furniture sitting about five feet away.

George likes chaos to some extent and was enjoying the spectacle. He said, "Hey, I think we still have our Christmas tree from last year, let's burn that while we're at it." He dragged over a terribly shabby, dried Christmas tree from the shed and threw it on the fireball, complete with old, dusty Christmas tree ornaments. They exploded in a myriad of directions. We were laughing pretty hard until we looked over and saw that Braden was rubbing his left hand and wincing. I examined his hand and saw it was covered with red marks. He'd been splashed by the boiling grease.

I put Braden in the sidecar of the motorcycle and drove him to the Sweetwater Medical Clinic. I had never driven a motorcycle before and didn't do too good of a job. It was definitely an adventure, though, and I'm all about that.

December 1992

Braden's brother (Huey) walked out of the photo on the family hallway wall and into Gumbeaux this week. He spotted me right away and said he recognized me from one of Braden's pictures. He said his name was Huey. He asked where Braden was, but I had no idea. Huey then asked me to sit with him while he had a drink in the bar. His breath and behavior indicated we may have been his third or fourth bar stop that evening. He sat down and ordered a dozen raw oysters on the half shell and a filthy dirty vodka martini (Willie can make a fine martini). It wasn't busy at all in my section, so I sat for a bit with Huey.

I told him that he had actually taken George and me out fishing a while back, but apparently we didn't make much of an impression. We talked for a while about his family. Huey was much more open than Braden. At one point Huey said, "Yeah, my father's housekeeper, she won't go upstairs."

"Why is that?" I asked.

"Our mother committed suicide in the bathroom. She drank a whole bottle of liquid drainer. She didn't even leave a note. I don't go home much. But yeah, Florence won't go in that room anymore, not since it happened. She's very superstitious and says she can see Mom's ghost. She says her ghost sits at her bureau in front of the bathroom mirror, endlessly putting on makeup. But she's a corpse, so no amount of makeup in the world is going to do any good. She was so beautiful, too. A real shame. I was ten. Braden was eight." Huey motioned for Willie to get him another drink.

No wonder Braden is so screwed up. It's understandable why he doesn't want to talk about it. We do have a lot in common, after all. Later that evening, when he came by my dorm room to see me, I had it decorated with about a million little votive candles. We're not allowed to light them in the dorm, but whatever. Who couldn't use a little sweetness and light? His expression was worth it; he looked at me the way he looks at Satchmo.

February 1993

Betty and I were hanging out after work on Wednesday night, studying for our philosophy test. We studied for a whole hour straight, so Bubba decided to reward us with a few rounds of tequila shots. Well, after drinking that, we were in no shape to study anymore. It was about nine o'clock, and Betty reminded me that it was ladies' night at Inertia, the hot dance club downtown. It used to be a movie theatre. Now they have a huge movie screen where they put up cool images as the music is playing and people are dancing around. The images and music don't really go together. I don't know what the projection facilitator is smoking.

We were still in our Gumbeaux T-shirts, but that didn't stop us from getting our dance on. We were slamming margaritas like they were iced tea. The manager came over to us while we were dancing and asked if we would like to dance in the cage. You would have thought Betty had won the lottery. She's all about being the center of attention and having men stare at her. She asked me to dance in the cage with her. It seemed like a good idea at the time. We got in the cage and started doing some really sexy dancing. It was all in fun. At one point, a guy came over and took some pictures of us. We were posing and vogueing and having a great time.

We woke up around noon with hangovers. We had missed the philosophy test. Betty called our philosophy professor and said we had both been involved in an incident and requested a make-up test. The professor laughed at her, told her to read the newspaper and hung up. What had happened? We ran down to the student union building to buy a paper. People were whistling at us as we passed. When we got the paper, I gasped. Betty squealed with delight. On the front page of the People About Town section was a huge color photo of the two of us in a compromising pose, dancing in a cage. You could clearly read "Gumbeaux" on our shirts, and I imagined Lulu's reaction. Oh no.

Betty bought all the papers they had. She was beaming with pride. "Don't you care about how this looks?" I asked. "Lulu is going to flip out."

"So what? Bubba will be thrilled to death. Besides, what gives? Why do you care? There are plenty of other restaurants we could go work in."

"But I like Gumbeaux. I like Clarence, Catherine and Willie."

"Do you think they'd miss you? Give it up, girl. We're white. They're only going to like you so much. Accept it."

I thought that was a terrible opinion but didn't say anything.

We were both scheduled to work that night, of course. When we walked in the door, it was mid-afternoon. Lulu was closing out the day shift, and Bubba was preparing for the night shift. I use the term 'preparing' loosely. He just watched Lulu do all the work. The office door was open and they both looked up. Lulu seemed really pissed off.

"Betty, Veronica, get in here," Lulu said. "Bubba and I want to talk to you." We went into the little office. She told us to close the door, which was not a good sign. "Well, girls, it seems that you had quite a night." She slapped the paper down across her desk. Bubba was just standing by the door, watching. "I normally would consider this none of my business. However, you are wearing Gumbeaux T-shirts in the picture." I felt terrible and looked at the floor. Betty looked bored and was playing with her blond—I mean golden—hair.

"This is not the image we're looking to have," continued Lulu. "This is a family restaurant."

"No it isn't, Lulu," said Bubba. "You just want it to be. It's only a family restaurant while you're here. It's a bar when I'm here."

Lulu sneered at her husband. "If you insist on undermining my decisions, Bubba, then we don't have much of a partnership. You know I have a problem with this. Employees do not need to be photographed in our Gumbeaux shirts while participating in questionable activity."

I wanted to tell Lulu that if she thought this was bad, then she should come by some night and check out Betty distributing her signed centerfolds. I couldn't sell Betty down the river like that, though.

"None of the people who come here at night care about stuff like that," Bubba scoffed.

"Well, I care, and my friends care! I had to hear about this from the pastor's wife. It's an embarrassment!" Lulu was getting really red faced.

"Yeah, but what does that mean? That you don't get to sit on the front row pew? They made the paper wearing our shirts and that is free publicity. Advertising is advertising, Lulu."

Betty and I didn't know what to do. They were starting to get really upset—with each other.

"I've worked very hard to turn this place into a respectable establishment. I balance the books and have to fix them every day after you screw them up at night. And that's what you are. A screw-up. Your mother was right about you."

"Don't you dare bring my mother into this," Bubba shouted. "I've had it with your sanctimonious, pious crap. You didn't even care about all this God stuff until five years ago. Honey, God doesn't want you to be humorless, frigid and angry, He wants you to enjoy life and be happy. Why can't you find a church that believes in that? I could get behind if it wasn't so joyless. These girls were just having a good time. What's the big deal?"

The look on Lulu's face was really awful. "Girls, leave us." She didn't have to tell me twice, I was ready to bail the second Bubba dropped the word "frigid". I was as nervous as a long-tailed cat in a room full of rocking chairs and took off with Betty in tow. We went outside on the terrace. Sue Bell, the night supervisor, was outside smoking cigarettes and drinking coffee in preparation for the evening shift.

"Woo-wee, you girls are bad. Full of p and v—piss and vinegar," Sue Bell informed us. You could tell she loved the drama. "Lulu almost blew a gasket, believe you me. I tried to tell her girls will be girls. But she's a real hard ass nowadays."

"Did you see the picture?" cried Betty. "I thought we looked awesome! I can't wait to show my parents!"

Some people have parents who appreciate that kind of passion for living. Others of us absolutely do not. Thank goodness Claude lives like ten states away. What a scandal. Clarence, Catherine and Willie came outside to join us.

"Come on, child," Willie scolded me. "What are you thinking? Now you opened a door you can't shut. Some stuff may walk in that door you don't want to come in, darlin'."

"Cut it out, Willie," Betty said defensively. "You're scaring her."

"Betty, you're crazy. Veronica ain't like you. She's a nice girl. She thinks she wants to be a bad girl, but she ain't cut out for all that. Not really." Willie adjusted the toothpick in his mouth.

"Thanks," I mumbled.

"Thanks, my ass," yelled Catherine. "You're not innocent, girl, not by a long stretch. It's your own selfishness that gets you into trouble."

"Selfishness?" I was surprised by Catherine's outburst.

"Yes, selfishness. Selfish ass selfishness. You know better than to act a fool while wearing Gumbeaux shirts. This place has been good to both of you. Lulu and Bubba have been good to you. I've worked in a whole mess of restaurants, and they're good people. I know they whine and make noise, but they're good people just the same. And you done them wrong. You know you did. You were too busy thinking of your own self and having a good old time. Selfish, selfish, selfish." Both Catherine and Willie were on a tear.

Catherine turned to Betty. "And you. Don't even get me started. You have done nothing but lead this girl down a bad path from day one. You pose in *Playboy* magazine and then show the customers to get your tips way up there. You act like you Miss Louisiana but you ain't. You act like the town cruise director, but you ain't. You ain't no lady. Everybody know you a skanky ho."

"I am not a skanky ho!" Betty was highly offended.

"All right, that's it!" yelled Willie, swinging his fat arms around. "We've got enough fightin' indoors; we came out here to get away from all that!"

"Are they really fighting?" asked Sue Bell, not even trying to conceal her delight.

"Yeah, Sue Bell, they're fightin' all right. Don't know why you're so happy about it, you stupid polecat." Willie turned to me. "What's wrong with you, girl?"

Lots, for sure, but the specifics are anyone's guess. I really wanted to ask Willie what a polecat was but it wasn't the time.

"Yeah," agreed Catherine. "What's wrong with you? What if they get so mad they get divorced and close the restaurant? I got my kids to take care of, I'm a single momma. If you screw up my job, we're going to have problems, you and me." She did some weird hand gesture that made Willie shudder. It appeared to be a voodoo hex. Great. Like I don't have enough problems without a disciple of voodoo casting spells on me. She stormed back inside and slammed the door. Betty gave me a look that said, *I told you so*.

"Don't worry, darlin'," said Sue Bell. "She don't really know no voodoo. She just read a coupla books about it at the library, so all of a sudden she thinks she's Marie Laveau or some shit."

It was a long night. Lulu left in a huff, Bubba drank triple his usual amount and no one felt very productive. I asked Willie if he had any wisdom to impart. He shrugged and said, "Girl, ain't no surprises here. Sheeeeeeeit. When you lie with the dogs, you get fleas."

So now I'm back in the dorm room, picking off fleas and watching Betty cut out our newspaper article for her scrapbook. Today I got a call from Bubba. He was hemming and hawing and said it might be good if Betty and I took a month's long leave of absence from Gumbeaux. We could come back at that time, once tempers had cooled.

Braden said not to sweat the whole Gumbeaux thing. His response was, "Sweetheart, I've lost like five jobs this year *alone*. Who cares? It's the restaurant business. You're *supposed* to be transient and get fired all the time. Just work down the street at The Steak Pit."

But Gumbeaux is special. I don't want to work anywhere else.

February 1993

I've started a series of Louisiana inspired paintings. The first set is of the marshes and wetlands of Grand Isle. The second set is of majestic brown pelicans taking flight, low to the water, with the setting sun giving a mysterious and shadowy backdrop.

Braden talked me into making good use of my newfound unemployment. He wanted us to spend some time traveling around the state. He said Louisiana history class was fine and good, but the only way to really understand Sportsman's Paradise was to experience it firsthand. The first place we went to was Natchitoches, several hours north of Bayou Bend. Braden said Natchitoches, or "Nack" as he called it, is the oldest city in Louisiana and the original colony in Louisiana about 1714. I asked him to show me the Melrose Plantation along the Cane River while we were there. He said I had the wrong guy and to call George for outings of that nature. He did give me a brochure, though.

The town of Natchitoches (pronounced Nack-a-tish, a Natchitoches Indian word meaning "place of the Paw Paw" or "Chinkapin") is the oldest permanent settlement in Louisiana. Founded in 1714 to promote trade with the local Indians and the Spanish in Mexico, Natchitoches played a major role in the history of Texas and Louisiana. The French first made contact with the Indians in the Natchitoches area in 1700. A friendly trade developed which led Governor Cadillac to extend that trade to the Spanish colonies in Mexico. In 1714, Cadillac sent his lieutenant Juchereau de St. Denis to establish a trading post at the head of the navigation on the Red River. That post grew into the town of Natchitoches.

Braden mentioned that while we were there, he had to "deliver something." It was probably guns or drugs or both. We met one of his thug friends in downtown Natchitoches at a charming little café at the river's edge. There were signed photos of Julia Roberts on the wall, as well as the cast from the movie *Steel Magnolias*, which had scenes filmed in Natchitoches. While Braden and his henchman quietly hatched plans of bad intent, I went outside and walked up and down the street. I could tell where the Easter scene at the end of the movie was filmed, which inspired me to begin reciting some of the movie lines. When I turned around, a couple of women in elaborate hats were standing behind me, smiling. They looked as though they had just gotten out of church. They did not seem to find it odd at all to happen upon someone quoting movie lines to herself, which was a relief.

"We met her, you know," one of them said.

"Met... who?" I asked.

"Julia Roberts, of course. She was here filming the movie. We both met her." You could tell she wanted to be asked a lot of questions about the event, but there was no way I was going to indulge her.

"Yep, we met her," put in her friend, wanting to ensure that her brush with fame was also acknowledged.

"She wasn't very nice, though," said the other lady, wrinkling up her pert little nose and patting her newly coiffed hair.

"I thought she was nice," said the friend. "She was actually very nice. Maybe she just wasn't nice to you. Maybe she didn't like you."

I backed away from this conversation and quickly returned to Braden and what was sure to become a crime scene. They were just wrapping things up. Evening was settling in, and the sky looked like orange juice with a splash of cranberry. Braden said we would be camping in the Kisatchie National Forest, feeding alligators at the alligator park and watching buffalo roam around at the Adai Indian Nation Cultural Center.

We drove through bayous, forests, swamps and small towns. Braden took me to backwoods juke joints; he knows all the speakeasy saloons. Near Alexandria, he took me to a place called the Rising Sun, an old shotgun house that had been converted into a bar with backyard seating. Near Houma, we rented a custom aluminum airboat powered by a 454 cubic engine. I asked what we were doing. He said we were going deep into the swamps. I was scared that we'd get stuck, but he laughed.

"Not in this boat," he said. "Look at it, it's an airboat. It can glide in mere inches of water."

Airboats are flat-bottomed boats that are powered by an aircraft engine and propeller. The engine, prop and seats are mounted high on the boat to raise the center of gravity so the boat will skim over the surface rather than having to push its way through the water. Braden started it right up and we glided from the dock slip out into the water. He seemed to know what he was doing.

"Now, once we get deep into the swamps, we're going to look for gators. We can feed them," Braden explained. Today's shirt had a picture of a Greek statue and read *Chiseled*.

"Feed them what? Our toes?"

"No, I brought some frozen chicken livers."

"I'm not going to play *Crocodile Dundee* with you," I said, trying to hide my terror.

"They aren't crocs, they're gators. Read your Louisiana history books again," Braden cackled in an Australian accent, ever the actor.

"I don't want to go where the wild things are."

"Of course you do. You love it, and you know you love it. You just need me to give you the courage," he encouraged. "We're going. Get ready for some action. You'll need a gun. Maybe you can borrow that gun from your Barbie doll." He laughed himself nauseous as I shook my head wearily. He thought the gun Dante gave me was "weak sauce."

"We're not killing anything, are we?" I wanted to know.

"I don't know. Maybe. If we find ourselves in a kill or be killed situation, then, yeah. If we feel threatened, yes. If we think there has been any cause for concern, then yes. If someone looks at us the wrong way, then, of course we would." He was just screwing with me as usual.

The swamps were teeming with life. We saw a lot of herons, egrets, turtles, fish and snakes. At one point I looked up and gasped. There was a huge nest way up in a tree, as large as a child's tree house. At the edge of the nest, looking down at us was an enormous bald eagle. We could tell from its body language that it considered us too close to the nest. I gestured to Braden and pointed at the eagle. Braden looked up, saw it and uttered several expletives as he began back paddling to put additional space between our canoe and the eagle. It didn't make any noise, but the babies in the nest were really squawking. We couldn't see them, but we could hear them and we knew they were there. Braden asked if I saw the size of its talons, but who could miss them? What was a bald eagle doing here in a Louisiana swamp? Shouldn't it be flying around places like Colorado and Montana? Apparently eagles can adapt and live wherever they want. The eagle never left its perch, but it certainly watched us until we got out of sight.

The cabin where we stayed was very modest, clean and snug. Not long after sunset, the moon rose into the sky. It was a gorgeous parchment paper yellow. It was so close that it had to be affecting tides somewhere. Braden wanted to get in the water and go skinny dipping. After a couple of bottles of wine, anything sounds like a great idea.

After a few minutes, I noticed something in the water. It was an object swimming about fifteen feet away from us, and it looked like a small dog. Knowing how he is about Satchmo, I asked if we should try to save it. Braden's eyes got big and he said no. Then he got back up on the dock lightning fast and pulled me back up with him. He took my arm and led me back to the house. He didn't want to tell me what it was. Finally, he confessed that it was a nutria rat, an enormous swamp rat. I screamed so loud that lights started to go on in cabins all around the lake. When all was peaceful again, he told me that some people actually eat nutria rats. More screaming ensued.

It was a pretty fun trip. The only real downside was that Braden said he thought we were very good together and that he could see our relationship going somewhere. That came as an unpleasant surprise and seemed positively surreal. Being with him is only possible in small doses; it's like **flying too close to the sun.** Braden is a blinding, burning force of life. Swinging from a star is quite a thrill ride, but who can sustain that?

March 1993

Recovering from the most terrifying night of my life. Tonight while we were visiting Satchmo at the Cypress Auto Parts junkyard, a bunch of gang members broke in with the intent of stealing motorcycle engines. Satchmo attacked one of them and practically tore his face off. The other four managed to shut him into an office, so Braden and I were on our own.

We ran through the junkyard and hid for a while, but they found us. Braden tried to fight them off and got in several good punches, but they held him down and tied his hands behind his back. They whispered amongst themselves as I cowered against Braden. It turned out that these men were in an infamous local motorcycle gang called the Sons of Darkness. Why couldn't it have been Clarence the busboy and his gang? They would have probably let us off with a warning. Not these guys, though. They were looking at Braden like a prize racehorse and at me like chattel. They didn't even address me directly, like I didn't really count as a person. My whole body trembled the entire time, there was no stopping it. Sue Bell's sister and her cautionary tale kept coming to mind.

The Sons of Darkness threw us both in the trunk of a car and drove us to a backwoods bayou weekend fight night event they had going on. They pulled us out of the car and we saw that there were thirty more of them to deal with. The gang was comprised of dirty, greasy guys who looked like they worked on active offshore oilrigs when not doing this. Somehow they knew Braden was a boxer. Apparently, this town is so small that even the gang members know what's going on. They wanted their best fighter to go up against Braden. They had this makeshift boxing ring they had put together. They told Braden that if he lost, they were going to keep me as a trophy.

The fight was a pretty bad fight. It was scarier than anything I could ever dream up in my own head. It was some Stephen King stuff, believe you me. I thought we were goners for sure. Braden was beaten up and bloody, but just when I thought he had given up he came back and crushed their warrior. When Braden walked out of the ring, I couldn't see the other guy's chest rise any more. I looked away.

Braden came over to where I was being watched by a few gang members. They were making sure I didn't leave. One of them left an oily handprint on my arm that I didn't even see until later. They released me into Braden's custody and we walked away. The crowd didn't do anything to stop us. They let us go. They parted to let us out and everything. I guess they were in awe of Braden, but I'm not—not anymore. I just want out. I may like to flirt with danger, but almost getting gang raped by it is another thing entirely.

All I want to do is put this night behind me and forget about it forever. But for some reason this black, oily handprint on my arm won't come off. I've been scrubbing and scrubbing, but I just can't get it all the way off.

March 1993

Braden Davis has left Louisiana. No one filed any complaints, there were no reports. Instead, Braden was simply advised by the Sons of Darkness via messenger that he had a week to get out of the area, and that he should stay away for at least a year or two.

Then there was the business of Satchmo, which had actually made local news. Betty grabbed me in the middle of taking an order and dragged me over to the television in the bar area. A Bayou Bend reporter was interviewing both Braden and Earl, the owner of Cypress Auto Parts. Earl told the reporter how Braden and his girlfriend were on the property when burglars broke in. Earl described how the burglars trapped his guard dog, Satchmo, in the front office. Satchmo had fought so viciously to escape the office that he broke his canine teeth with the effort of smashing open the metal door. The camera then closed in on Satchmo's brand new $3,000.00 titanium fangs, purchased for him by none other than Braden Davis.

Betty and I both gasped at the image of the Belgian Malinois with metal capped canines. Satchmo was more terrifying than ever, and seemed to be smiling, proudly displaying his grin. It reminded me of the villain 'Jaws' from *Moonraker.* His image was absolutely riveting. He was sitting obediently next to Braden and looking up at him in adoration. Braden would now be the custodian of Satchmo, because Earl was selling Cypress Auto Parts as soon as possible. He said that he was tired of the stress and the riffraff issues, and that Satchmo had earned an early retirement so that he could enjoy the rest of his life as a pet. If anyone could make a pet out of that hellhound, it was Braden, all right. The reporter asked what happened to his girlfriend. Braden got a faraway look in his eye and answered, "No comment."

Soon afterwards, Braden moved away to Los Angeles to try his luck there as an actor. Mr. Fitzgerald hooked him up with some talent agent, and so that's what he decided to do. He took his casino winnings and lit out for the territory. I feel a lot better knowing that at least he won't be alone out there. All is as it should be. Braden should be where the other stars are. He was a big fish in a small pond here in Bayou Bend. Now he's off to try his luck in the ocean of opportunity that is Hollywood land. If he gets the right kind of sponsors, he'll be sure to make it. I can't even explain the emptiness I feel to know that he's gone. I doubt that I will ever see him again.

5 GRADUATION

May 1993

There's not much to report as of late. After the motorcycle gang experience, all I did for a while was hang out in my dorm room and read. I ordered a lot of pizza because I was too nervous to go anywhere. After a little soul searching, I decided it was time to move out of the dorm.

I rented a little cottage just a couple of blocks away from the school. It has an herb garden outside the kitchen. Basil, parsley, mint, lavender and lemongrass perfume the outside air. I like to hang my sheets outside to dry so they absorb all the wonderful scents of the garden. Having fresh herbs readily available has sharpened my culinary skills. I have been doing a lot of cooking, not just with Miss Catherine, but also on my own. George and Betty like to come over and pretend to be fancy food critics.

Betty and I have been volunteering for the last few weeks at a soup kitchen downtown. She was required to do it as part of her community service for a certain incident in which she was pulled over doing 75mph in a 40mph zone. She actually ended up enjoying the community service so much that she kept doing it, even when she didn't have to anymore. I started going with her and working a couple of shifts each week. There are a lot of kids that show up, and they are the reason I keep showing up. Many of them have parents that just aren't around, for whatever reason. One of the little boys said that if it were not for the soup kitchen, he would never have anything to eat. When I heard that, it stuck with me for days afterwards. I finally prayed about it, because it seemed like the only way to get it out of my head. I prayed for the kid, and all the kids like him.

May1993

Graduation is next week. It's incredible how time flies. I forgot to order the cap and gown when I was supposed to do so, and ran into the student store in a panic and asked if there were any leftover caps and gowns from last year. The lady who runs the store winked at me, turned around and took a hanging bag off a rack behind her desk. It had a card on it with my name. I just looked at her in shock. She smiled and said, "We figured you were about a size six, Veronica." How did she know that? I was a size four upon arrival, but there's always free jambalaya around.

She handed me the cap and gown. I burst into tears and hugged her. "Thank you. This school has been so nice to me. Thank you, thank you."

This experience just sums up the way the south has felt to me. It feels like a hug.

I saw Dr. Landry when I was leaving the library. "I heard Braden moved to Hollywood to become a movie star," he told me with what sounded an awful lot like mock sympathy. "How are you holding up?"

I laughed. "Oh, I'll probably survive." **The girls of the south have taught me well. Such inquiries are best met with an easy, breezy response. Dr. Landry doesn't need to know** how much I miss Braden. I waved gaily and started to go.

"Veronica, wait a minute." Dr. Landry gently put out his arm to stop me. "Do you remember that talk we had at my house?"

"Maybe I do, and maybe I don't," I replied with a bit of a head toss. "It depends on what you're going to say next."

He chuckled and seemed to think my impertinence was cute. "I said I was going to check in with you when you graduated. That's in a week, so . . . this is me asking."

"Asking what?"

"Asking to see if you would still be interested in having crème brulée with me." His eyes were twinkling and something inside me melted. He wasn't just trying to get rid of me that time at his house. He wanted me around, even if he did send me packing to the theatre. Anything is possible. This is America.

"Sure, why not? I like crème brulee," I told him in a casual and polite sort of way. My heart rate was picking up, and it was all I could do it play it cool.

"Good," he said, eyes crinkling with warmth at their corners. "Glad to hear it. And I'm proud of you, by the way. Your grades were better this last semester than ever, and the student assistants really like working with you."

"Thank you. I'll really miss it here," I told him.

"Then don't leave." His voice was almost a caress; it made me feel like the most beautiful woman in the world.

Later that night, Willie, Betty and I were having a discussion. All the waitresses invariably would tell Willie their darkest secrets, and he would impart pearls of wisdom. Betty was complaining about her last boyfriend, the one from the hammer incident. She was saying that she really wanted him back, but he had not only changed his phone number, but moved and left no forwarding address. Willie told her, "Well, now, what that gonna tell ya, darlin'?" I started laughing and Betty got mad.

"Shut up, Willie," Betty threw a coaster in the shape of a crawfish at him. "I don't need to be told how to live my life by you. Mister oyster shucker man!"

"Then why you are you always tellin' me your business, girl? Sheeeeit." Willie didn't care one way or another; he was just making conversation as he shucked oysters. Oyster shucking can be a lonely business.

When I went home, I was shocked to find Claude parked outside, sitting in a red Lamborghini. Enough said.

"How did you find out where I live?" I was very shaken up.

"Mary. You're not exactly in witness protection, and you didn't exactly go to outer space." Claude opened the door and fell out of his car (where he rented a Lamborghini around here is beyond me), but somehow recovered with catlike agility. "Bayou Bend is a small town. You're not invisible, as much as you would like to think so."

Claude smelled like a brewery and was being exceptionally slurry, even for him. I invited him in the house because it seemed like the Southern thing to do. He analyzed my place and was very liberal with his criticism. Then he went rummaging around for liquor, like a bear making its way through a campsite. He found a bottle of cognac in my pantry. "Claude, you don't want to drink that; I just use it for making peppercorn sauce to go on steaks. It's sludge.

Don't you want a highball glass? You're really going to drink that out of a plastic cup?"

He filled his plastic cup full of ice cubes and knocked off a couple of my refrigerator magnets with his intensity in shutting the freezer. "I just figured people in Louisiana didn't know any better," he scoffed, pouring cheap cognac over the ice. You would have mistaken it for iced tea, had you seen it.

"You're the ignorant one," I replied, "if that's what you think. You wouldn't believe all the effort that goes into a Sazerac cocktail or a Pink Squirrel."

"Pink Squirrel? I've never heard of a Pink Squirrel," he murmured, knitting his eyebrows together in bewilderment.

"Well, that's probably the only drink you don't know." I pulled a tablecloth off a cart to reveal the wet bar. Betty and I had set it up, and there was nothing missing. Claude's mouth dropped open. "Here, let me hook you up, Claude," I told him with passive aggressive cheer. What will it be? A Colorado Bulldog? A Sadomasochist? An Early Christmas? You name it. If I don't know how to do it, I'll call my bartender friend, Willie, and he can walk me through the steps."

"Mary, since when do you know so much about alcohol? You don't drink." He looked at his own glass and actually put it down, as if in horror. There is a first time for everything.

"I do drink. You have driven me to drink. Congratulations. I even work in a restaurant with a bar in it." I beamed at him like a game show hostess about to gift him with a trip to Las Vegas.

He looked guilty, then disappointed, then furious. "Great. So, now you're an alcoholic."

"Hey, now—I think you're jumping a couple notches. I'm not an alcoholic, Claude. Alcoholics go to meetings, and I've certainly never done that." I laughed out loud. For some reason, he just wasn't getting to me anymore.

He seemed to sense a disturbance in the force. "Wow! Who knows what else you've been doing down here? You've always had a wild streak a mile wide. I could see it, which is why I always kept you under heavy surveillance. You are a little tart, aren't you? I wonder what your mother was like at your age. Do you think she was a tart too?"

That was really low. If he was trying to get a reaction, then it worked. I snatched one of my fireplace andirons and brought it sharply against his throat. "Did you really just ask me that?" I hissed. He was gagging, but I didn't care. "The only reason you still exist is because I've been too much of a coward to ever pull the trigger." His eyes got big. I turned the poker into his neck a little more, branding him with inky black soot. "Nobody here knows who you are, and nobody cares. Your connections, power and money can't help you right now, can they? And to be honest with you, I've dreamed of offing you for years. After you said I couldn't attend regular school anymore and had to be home schooled, I bought some glass crushed into powder and thought about putting it in your Vichyssoise. But you never got up to go to the bathroom, so you lived. And when we got snowed in that time at Capitol Hill? You passed out on the front steps, drunk as usual. I almost left you outside in the snow to freeze to death. We had these huge icicles on the roof that would have been perfect backup murder weapons. You're still alive because I didn't know how to kill you and get away with it. But I could do it now. There are people here who would help me cover it up and no one would miss you." I released my grip on his throat and he backed up, choking for air.

"Mary! Are you insane? What's happened to you?" he yelled, genuinely afraid. Like most bullies, he just needed someone to stand up to him. I really wished Braden was there. He would have been so proud.

"What's happened is that I'm getting better. Healthy people don't tolerate unhealthy behavior." I gestured menacingly at him with the poker, and he shuddered like a little girl. "All I want is my freedom, Claude. Why is that so hard to understand? I just want to find peace. You can't help me with this quest because you're a big part of the problem. Please, just leave me alone. The wound left from Mom and Dad dying hasn't scarred over yet. It's still open. I need time to heal and convalesce. And you want to rip it back open and throw salt on it. No. I won't let you hurt me anymore. If you don't back off, I promise I will have you taken out or maybe even do it myself. So stay away from me so I can grieve in peace and get better."

I put the poker back in its stand. "You can go now, but remember, you're on notice." I told him he was not welcome and never to come back again. He didn't argue and left. He looked strangely pale, almost green. Looks like the alcohol is starting to get to him physically, as well as mentally.

May 1993

Graduation day ended up being pretty wonderful, but it didn't start out that way. I didn't have any family taking pictures or whatever. When the ceremony was over, everyone else threw their caps in the air because they were excited to enter the next phase of their lives. I just clung to mine like a security blanket, scared to let go.

Putting an andiron up to Claude's throat meant moving home was off the table. I was sitting alone in the gym, where commencement had been held. Most of the people had already left to have dinner with their families. I just sat on one of the bleachers for a while, thinking that this was probably the last time I'd be there, maybe ever. Four years. Don't they go by in a blink? It was time to leave, and then I saw Dr. Landry was standing in the doorway, waiting for me. It had been raining, but you could see the sunshine through the rain, and it lit up the area around him. There was a sunset colored glow around his commencement robe, giving him an angelic aura. I walked over to him and smiled into his green and gold eyes.

"Hi," I said sheepishly.

"Hi," he said back. "Happy graduation day. What are you doing later?"

The years I had waited were over, and the effect of his presence was disconcerting. "Wow, Dr. Landry. You have less game than any man I have ever met. You could have just stuck your business card in my diploma before you handed it to me. That would be very efficient." It was my weak attempt at being mean to him and he didn't even seem to notice.

"Very funny, smart ass. Well, up until now you were a student, and dating you would have been against the rules. But now you aren't a student anymore." He looked so handsome in his academic robes. He kind of resembled a priest, though, which added a whole different dynamic to the exchange.

"It's still going to look bad, even though I just graduated," I said, thinking about the 1990 Award for Ethical Excellence plaque on his office wall.

"That's beyond my control." He leaned over and kissed me. I turned bright red because the Dean of Students was walking by and you could tell he'd seen it. He looked very surprised. Dr. Landry just smiled at him warmly, shrugged, took my hand and we left for his car. In the passenger seat was a wine bucket full of ice and a bottle of Dom Pérignon. I realized it was the bottle he has been saving for a special occasion. It felt wonderful to be his special occasion.

It was a long night. At one point when we were taking a bath, he was holding me close, kissing me, washing my hair, whispering, "Oh, Veronica. I could do this *forever*."

I felt the same way, and forever wouldn't be long enough. But I was far too shy to say anything of the sort, so I turned my hair into a big foamy shampoo Mohawk; and he laughed and told me I was worse than a child.

June 1993

I've secured enough work painting murals for local businesses that I was able to stop waiting tables. When I told Lulu and Bubba that I would be resigning, they had different reactions. Lulu was very professional and offered to write a letter of recommendation. Bubba started planning my farewell party, mainly because he's always ready for a party. The party was last night, and Willie, Clarence, Sue Bell, Betty, Lulu, Bubba and all the waitresses were there. Betty had put together a slide show of all of our adventures. We laughed and laughed and cried and cried. We drank too much and ate too much and had an outpouring of love.

There was a big surprise, too. Gumbeaux was for sale. Lulu and Bubba were retiring from the restaurant business, so they could work on their marriage. They wanted to pursue their own interests. Neither of them really liked the restaurant industry. Lulu wanted to work with her church and Bubba wanted to be a professional New Orleans tour guide. Willie had made them an offer on the restaurant. He was buying it from them and making Catherine and Clarence his business partners. This announcement, and the smile on Willie's face, really made all of us happy. The restaurant was going to be in good hands. I asked Clarence how Willie got the money to buy the restaurant. He winked and told me that Willie had been collecting pearls from the oysters that he shucked for about twenty years. When he finally cashed them in, he had enough for a significant down payment and an offer that Lulu and Bubba couldn't refuse.

At one point, when things were winding down, I took one last look around Gumbeaux. A lot of wonderful experiences have taken place here. It has been like being in a big, happy, dysfunctional family. A huge mess. I looked at all the pictures on the walls, the spices on the shelves, Catherine's gumbo pots, the walk-in chiller that Braden and I desecrated that one day and outside by the trees in the back parking lot. I looked out to the dumpsters one last time and gasped at what I saw. My crow was on the ground next to the dumpster. He had a broken wing and was walking around in a circle. He was limping around, not making any noise. He was just breathing in chokes. I ran over to see him more closely, but he went around the back of the dumpster. When I got there, he was gone. I ran around the dumpster a couple more times, and then looked up to see Clarence shaking his head at me.

"You need a head doctor, you a mental case, girl." Then he offered me a Kool menthol cigarette. I don't even smoke but actually accepted one this time, mainly to be polite. I took one puff and started gagging.

"This tastes like eucalyptus and Freon," I gasped. He said that these were the light ones, and that I should try the regulars if I thought these were bad. I asked if he was going to keep working at Gumbeaux.

"I don't have a lot of options. This is the best one I have so far, so yeah. Until I get a BBD," Clarence replied.

"BBD? What's a BBD?" I wanted to know.

"A bigger better deal," he said.

"Oh, okay. Would you move away from Bayou Bend for a bigger better deal?" I wanted to know.

"Yeah, the bigger the BBD, the further I would be willing to move. That's the way the world works, Ron." He seemed supremely confident that there were BBDs waiting for him around every corner.

"One day I hope to call you and offer you the BBD of a lifetime," I told him.

"Yeah, me too, girl. I hope you don't be branding your help, either." He pulled up his arm and showed me his brand. "This gang isn't even around anymore, and I have this ugly ass thing on my arm, probably forever. Can you believe that? Just goes to show you that the need to belong is stronger for some than others." He started laughing and I had to join him. It was so good to sit there outside with Clarence, laughing at our misspent youth until tears ran down our faces.

I went back inside to the waning party. Betty was helping box up the cake. She had really given me a nice party. I went over to give her a hug and thank her.

"Where were you?" she asked. "You missed it. Dr. Landry was just here and asked where you were."

"And he's already disappeared?"

"Yeah. Just like that. He was here, and then gone again." Betty shrugged.

"Houdini has nothing on Dr. Landry," I agreed.

"Hey, now that you're dating him, don't you think you should start calling him Richard?" asked Betty with a girlish giggle.

I turned bright red. "That's so wrong."

"It might be wrong, but when I'm right, I'm right. Look at you. You're glowing," she said. "Besides, I saw your car in his driveway." She put her arm around me. "What's the problem, Ronnie? You should be proud of yourself! You bagged the elephant. He's what you always wanted."

Well, sure. The relationship makes sense. For some reason, though, I can't stop thinking about Braden.

July 1993

The mural work is holding steady. I recently finished a job with the City of Bayou Bend. They asked me to paint the entryway of the Convention and Visitors Bureau. They said I could design whatever I wanted, but you have to take that kind of freedom with a grain of salt and practice a little discretion. Carte blanche on someone else's dime is not really carte blanche. That being the case, I tried to be very respectful of their marketing needs. I spent hours at the library looking for popular images of the south. Nothing seemed to jump out at me, so I went home and watched the *Gone with the Wind*. During the scene where Scarlett goes to Ashley Wilkes' party at Twelve Oaks, I had an epiphany. The image of the trees in front of the plantation home resonated in my brain, as if someone had activated a tuning fork there.

For the entryway of the Convention and Visitors Bureau, I designed a series of mysterious oak trees with Spanish moss gently descending from them. The branches almost seemed animated, and gold leaves were woven throughout the green foliage in a few strategic places. The sky above became obscured by green canopy. It took me weeks to finish the job. We had agreed upon the amount up front. By the time I completed the project and figured out my cost of labor per hour, it was barely minimum wage. That was my choice, though. It didn't have to be as good as I made it, but that was part of the fun. I wanted it be something that the people of Bayou Bend would be proud of. George and Betty and Richard would see it, and so would visitors from outside the area. I wanted to make them look good.

It was very taxing physically. Although a few people expressed concern that I might be a workaholic, Richard wasn't one of them. The one time I whined about biting off more than I could chew, he just smiled. "It's good for you. Keep at it. Besides, you should make it the best that it can possibly be. After all – your name is going to be on it."

After he said that, I worked twice as hard and it ended up exceeding my expectations. I completed the ceiling Michangelo style, lying on my back on a series of catwalks. A mini-Sistine Chapel. I've been able to leave an imprint, however faint, on Bayou Bend. There's something that stirs the soul in Spanish moss gently rustling through tree branches at twilight. The way a full moon reflects on the Mississippi River. The spirit and fire in the people here. Passion, joie de vivre and love are like ingredients in the gumbo that is life here. Most of all, it's the love. I've lived so much here, lost so much here and loved so much here. And really, since my life was so sheltered before, I grew up here. Everyone I know from work and from school has had a hand in that, and I am grateful for every last one of them.

August 1993

Braden called Richard's house today, looking for me. When Richard handed me the phone, he looked as if someone had given him a dirty diaper. Braden said he was calling from Los Angeles. He had called Gumbeaux to get my number, and Betty had told him I was seeing Richard. I'm sure she enjoyed telling Braden that immensely. He asked if it was true, and I told him that it was. Braden seemed upset. He wanted me to "lose the old dude" and join him and Satchmo in Los Angeles. He said he had his Streamliner parked on various beaches, and that we could explore Southern California together. He told me that he had been learning to surf, and that he was a natural. He said that although he wasn't getting any good parts in Hollywood yet, that the dog was. As a result, Braden was spending most of his time driving Satchmo to his auditions.

It was really good to talk to Braden again, and a huge relief to know he was alive and well. But I was honest and told him that I didn't want to live a reckless, wild life any more. I thought that I did, and I thought I had what it took to tramp around the globe with him, but I didn't. Not really. I wanted some stability and normalcy. I had completely stopped being a party girl when I began dating Richard and didn't miss it at all. Besides, college was over, so it was time to grow up.

Braden told me that he was disappointed, but not surprised, and that he hoped we would always stay in touch. That was just something to say, though. Both of us were ready to have nothing to do with each other by the end of the call.

September 1993

It was a wonderful summer, one experience after another. On my birthday, Richard surprised me with a weekend in New Orleans. We saw Harry Connick Jr. perform live. He had an entire jazz band backing him up. A little old lady sitting next to me got out of her seat and started dancing, right there in the concert hall. Others joined suit, and then there were several hundred people up out of their chairs, having a wonderful time and celebrating the collective soul that is jazz. The next morning, we enjoyed fresh strawberries, eggs benedict, café au lait and seafood grits au gratin.

Richard has been a wonderful teacher in so many ways. He's helped me be much more confident. We talk for hours about ideas, thoughts, and concepts. He's a wonderful amateur psychologist and can break down my beliefs and fears. He has all the answers. I've never watched someone sleep before until now. It's an amazing thing to love someone from the bottom of your soul up. I know every little line on his face; every laugh line is etched into my soul. Each one of them is a reminder that he's mortal and will also die, and each time his chest moves is an affirmation that when that stops, he won't be there anymore. Maybe this is how people feel about their children. There's no telling how long this will last. Every second is precious. Lots of other things in life have been mediocre, for sure, but never a second of the time spent with him. It will always be important, somehow I know this.

Something deep down tells me that Richard might not like my other life. I mean, he would, but he wouldn't. So maybe it's better that he never finds out. I'll just get a normal job working at a museum in New Orleans or something. Claude will be the steward of Musée Fait for many years to come, it's not like he's going anywhere.

I got to tag along on the art club's annual trip to Europe. This year the club went to Paris for a week. One night we had dinner at an old standard, Brasserie Balzar. Frommers describes it as battered but cheerful. I'd describe the menu as upscale comfort food in an unpretentious setting. We had a great dinner. We'd been at the Degas Museum earlier. I ran into some colleagues on my way back from the bathroom. They wanted to know how things were going at Musée Fait. I spoke with them a couple of minutes, but turned around to see that Richard was behind me. I don't know what he heard but it couldn't have been good.

"Who are you, Veronica? Who are you, really? And don't tell me, 'nobody from nowhere' again." He wasn't kidding around. Richard expected an answer, but I was too scared to respond. He was pretty irritated and didn't talk much for the rest of the night. We flew home the next day. He hasn't brought it up since, but there isn't much more stalling time left. He's going to need an explanation, and it's going to be a difficult conversation. I'm too far down the rabbit hole now.

6 STEWARD

November 1993

Claude is dying.

Dante called and told me Claude is dying. It's quite a shock and absolutely numbing. He's dying of cancer. Apparently he has had it for five years. Claude never said a word about it. Dante said Claude believed he could beat cancer. Claude has been going through extreme chemotherapy, which explains his recent hair loss. All those years of plotting of his demise and here it is. I had the strangest reaction to the news—extreme nausea and vomiting. Dante waited patiently for me to get back on the phone, and then said at 1 p.m. there would be a private jet waiting for me at the airport.

Dante told me Claude had filled him in on the way he had treated me over the years. Apparently Claude had some kind of sudden realization about what a jerkoff he had been. I packed a bag and made a phone call.

"Hi," I said to Richard. "It's me."

"Hey, Veronica, is everything all right? Your voice sounds funny."

"Claude is incredibly sick. He's having renal failure. He had advanced cancer and I only just found out about it." The news was still a huge shock.

"That's terrible," Richard said. "Is there anything I can do for you?"

"Yes. Come with me to Washington," I requested.

The line went quiet for a moment. "What? Veronica, I can't just pick up and go to Washington. I've got like ten advisee meetings this afternoon; several people are counting on me to help them with their Basquiat papers. Do you know how expensive tickets are when you don't buy them thirty days in advance?"

"I've got a chartered jet. It's all taken care of. It won't cost you a cent. Please. I can't face this by myself. I'll show you D.C.; I know you want to see D.C. Everyone should go see D.C. at least once in their lifetime. It's a magnificent place. Please, Richard, please. Just for the weekend."

He was baffled. "A chartered jet? Why do you have a chartered jet?"

"Please," I implored. "I really need you. I'll do whatever you want."

"Don't say things like that, it's very distracting. I guess I could have my assistant reschedule my meetings. Okay, all right, fine. I'll go. I'll go. Why do you have a chartered jet? I can't believe I'm doing this. What time are we going?"

"Whenever you're ready. I'll come get you and we'll go to the airport. Can you be ready in, like, thirty minutes?"

"An hour would be better," he hedged.

"Oh come on, Richard, man up! I've gotten ready to go to an inauguration in thirty minutes."

"Uh huh. Was this when you became first lady of the nation? I'm not going if you're going to act like a princess the whole time."

"Sorry. I'll be there in an hour. Thank you, thank you, thank you. I'll make this so worth your while."

"Again, distracting. I'll go home and get some things together. How should I pack?" asked Richard.

"Same as you would here, but thirty or forty degrees cooler." He groaned when he heard that.

He was surprised to be collected in a stretch limousine complete with a one-hundred-year-old bottle of scotch. When we drove right up to the runway, he said we couldn't do that. Then he saw the jet waiting for us, and he was mortified. "I'm not getting on the plane until you answer some questions."

"Sure," I said, ready for anything. "Shoot."

"Why do you have a jet at your disposal?"

"We own it," I shrugged absently, focusing on Claude and the dilemma at hand.

"*Your family has its own jet?* That phone call about the Kimbell Museum—that was for real, wasn't it?" The professor demanded to know.

"Yes, it was for real. I'm connected to the Musée Fait."

"The Musée Fait? How are you connected to Musée Fait?" he asked, surprise evident in his face.

"Jean-Luc Fait was my grandfather."

"What?!" He gasped and turned somewhat pale.

"He was my grandfather," I confessed. "I changed the spelling from Fait to Fey to attend school at Audubon on the down low. My parents are gone, my grandmother is senile and my uncle is about to die. That leaves me as the last descendant of Jean-Luc Fait. So as soon as Uncle Claude is gone, I'll be the sole owner of Musée Fait."

"The owner? You own it? You own one of the most prestigious collections of art in America?" Richard was having a hard time wrapping his head around it.

"Yeah, pretty much. Musée Fait was my grandfather's house and art studio on Capitol Hill. Uncle Claude opened it to the public in 1983. I'm really sorry I didn't tell you before. I will inherit the museum and all the art when Claude dies. Everyone else is out so basically I'm inheriting it by default."

"But you're an infant, a child! You're in no way qualified to . . . oh, don't look at me like that; sorry if that hurt your feelings. Unbelievable. Why did you come to Louisiana? And why didn't we know who you were? I don't understand . . . "

"Richard, please. Ask whatever questions you want, but can we please just get on the plane?" I begged. "Claude doesn't have much time left. I have to see him before he dies."

He acquiesced. "Okay."

The whole way there, I didn't cry. It was very numbing, like watching it happening to someone else, like in a soap opera or something. Richard was pretty quiet, taking it all in. I was too busy discussing details with Dante to worry about what he was thinking.

November 1993

Claude looks terrible. It was kind of hard to recognize him tonight. He's probably never going to leave that hospital alive. He has a private room, a big screen TV, a stack of new magazines, a silver tray full of food—none of which looked like they had been touched at all.

He had paintings hanging on the walls of his hospital room. I was shocked to see that they were my paintings. They were all of the paintings I had sold during my first art show in Bayou Bend, the one where he showed up and tried to get me to leave with him for the Getty. I realized that I never did get to meet the mysterious benefactor who had bought the entire collection. Go figure. I was a little disappointed for a moment, but then realized that it didn't matter if Claude had been the one to buy all my paintings. The result of him doing so was that I started to believe in my talent. If I had known it was him, it would have been quite different. None of that mattered any more; it was all a moot point.

He was just lying there staring at the ceiling, looking absolutely defeated and petrified. His skin has turned green. He's lost a lot of hair. You can actually smell the cancer inside of him. What an insidious disease it is. It rots you from the inside out, same as jealousy.

Claude started bawling when he saw me. He apologized over and over, begging me to forgive him. He said he was terrified that he would go to hell for the way he had treated me. He really believed it; you could see the fear in his yellowed, bloodshot eyes. He asked if I would forgive him. I told him I had forgiven him even before he asked. That didn't sound like me at all, but that was my response.

Claude told me that he had never understood the difference between loving someone and controlling someone. He said that the times he had tried to control me, it was because he didn't want to see me get hurt. He said he knew he had hurt me anyway because of his excessive drinking. He said that the reason he had brought up my parents so frequently was not to torture me, but because he missed them so much. He said that he had always considered me a great artist. That was a hard-won validation of my talent and I got misty for a moment.

Claude then went on to say that artists often live dark lives and he never wanted that for me. He said the greatest artists often went to the Dark Side, and he was worried that if I descended, part of my soul could be lost forever.

I brushed off his ominous words with confidence. "You don't need to worry about that. I already went to the Dark Side, and now I've made it back." He looked peaceful after hearing that response, and hugged me for a long time. The hug was full of remorse and all the things that words couldn't say.

Before I left, Claude said that Dante had transferred everything over to me. He said it was all mine and I could do whatever I wanted now. He said to be really nice to the people at the Smithsonian because they had been so good to us over the years. It was so surreal.

I left Claude's hospital room at midnight. Richard was in the lobby, waiting for me and chatting with Dante. Dante had gotten us a black Lincoln Town Car and a driver. The driver would take Richard and me to Capitol Hill, to my house. We were finally alone in the back seat of the car. I put my hand over his. He was pretty quiet the whole way to our place. I had the driver pass by all the monuments on the way home. Richard's face lit up like a child at Christmas upon seeing the Washington, the Jefferson and Lincoln Memorials. I told him we'd visit them tomorrow, if he liked. I felt sure that he would love living in D.C. and would fit in beautifully. When we reached the house, he was startled by our home's proximity to the Capitol Building and the overall grandeur of the place.

The new butler greeted us at the private family entrance. There were about five dozen pale pink roses in the entry way. The staff knows they are my favorite. Once he was settled in, we went to the kitchen. The new cook (Claude's staff has high turnover) asked what we would like to have for dinner. I said we'd like ten-ounce ribeyes cooked medium rare, Belgian fries with truffle oil and steamed asparagus with béarnaise sauce. The cook whipped it up in about thirty minutes, as we shared a bottle of cabernet sauvignon in the library in front of a roaring fire. Richard was acting weird. Less confident than usual, quiet and a bit on guard.

After dinner, we went to the third floor which had been locked for years as Claude had forbidden me to unlock it. I got a bolt cutter and took off the dead bolt Claude had put on it. Then I went into the room. It was like a time capsule. It was my parents' suite, just the way they had left it. I went through their things, tears rolling down my face as I did. Tears of happiness. Claude hadn't thrown all their things away like he said he had. Mom's clothes were all still there. Each shirt, blouse and sweater brought back a different memory of her. It was so much all at once, it was just beautiful—and heart breaking.

Richard just watched me. He really knows when to say something and when to just sit there and listen. He just sat there and watched me heal. I sat next to him and he let me put my head on his chest, and I could hear his heart beating. It felt so good to be in his presence, a place of peace.

November 1993

I have never been so depressed in my life.

Dante called and said Claude had passed away. He would be over in the morning with a bunch of papers for me to sign. I hung up the phone and looked at Richard. We were sitting in the library. He had been going through our collection of art books.

"Claude is gone."

Richard nodded. "Wow."

"Wow is right."

"I heard Dante talking to you on the plane. All of this is yours now?" He seemed apprehensive and exhausted.

"Yeah," I admitted. "It really is."

"The Musée Fait?"

"That's right." I tried to hug him.

"Don't touch me," he growled. I was reminded of Satchmo.

"What? Why?" I was totally unprepared for his anger and took a step backward.

"Because I don't know who you are. All this while, you've had access to limitless resources. We should have given your scholarship to someone who actually needed it. You had millions at your disposal, and you chose the road less traveled to save your soul from an evil caretaker. Don't you think that's something you could have filled me in on?"

"Whatever," I replied. "It worked. You got me through it. I couldn't have done it without you."

"You're giving me too much credit. All I did was buy you a thousand cups of coffee." He was pretty mad.

"I'm not giving you too much credit, and I'd drink a thousand cups of bleach if that's what it took to be near you. I'll buy you a coffee bean plantation if that would make you happy. You're the only good man I know."

"You've been kept captive most of your life, you don't know anything," he said evenly, as if thinking aloud.

"I know that I love you. I do know that much." My cowardice seemed to have disappeared along with Claude's life force. "I love you, and I can't do this without you. I can't manage this without you."

"Veronica . . . "

"I need you, Richard. I want you to run the collection with me. Think about it. You're perfect for it. You know more about art than most people on the planet. And I can do so much for you. Do this with me, please."

"You don't want me to do it with you. You want me to do it *for* you." He folded his arms.

"That's so not true! We can do this together, as a team!"

"You have pretty good judgment; you don't need to rely on mine. You don't need me to think for you." He was pacing around the room, looking at various objets d'art. He was looking closely at them, unable to believe he was in the same room with them.

"Richard, no. You were just calling me an infant and a child who was in no way qualified, remember?"

He rubbed his forehead, probably anticipating a migraine. "Your deception may have been necessary, but I am not okay with it at all. You pretended not to know anything about art for years. You pretended not to know things you must have known."

"No, none of that is true."

"You told me that you thought Degas was from Samoa," He sneered.

I started laughing. "Well, obviously that was a joke."

"If I wasn't in on it, then it was only a joke to you. You don't need me. You just want me to be your Sherpa. Don't deny it."

"I'm sorry you feel that way, Richard, but it's just not true. The truth is I was assuming a new life. I told you that if I didn't get away from Claude, I was going to kill him. I didn't want to do that. I mean, I did, but I didn't want to go to jail or have to meet the consequences of killing him. So I ran away. And running away brought me to you. And I'm glad and grateful! But I get that you probably need to stay in Louisiana, so if you won't come to Musée Fait, then it shall come to you. I'll move the whole thing to New Orleans. We'll do it brick by brick if necessary. Granddad loved New Orleans, and I'm sure he would have approved."

"What? No." He shook his head for emphasis. "Listen to yourself, V. You can't make rash decisions like that as a leader. You don't even realize what you're saying. You probably have people employed here in town, right? You haven't even hesitated to think about all the lives you'd be disrupting by moving such a significant organization out of here. You're the boss now. Your employees are counting on you for their livelihoods, and you're responsible for them."

"See? I do need you; my judgment isn't good at all, it sucks. I'm a bad person without you. You understand how to take care of me on a psychological level and I'll do what you say. You can be the man behind the curtain. You'll have no limits as far as artistic resources. I can make your art famous just by having it here in the museum, and you'll go down in history as an important painter." Honestly, I was willing to do anything to have Richard stay with me. You don't want to know how far I'd go.

"That's some hard bait to refuse, but I'm not taking it." Richard looked depressed and older than usual. "I'd like to get back to Bayou Bend, if your big fancy jet is available. This hasn't gone quite as I'd hoped."

"Don't be so quick to answer, Richard. Let the idea marinate in your head for a while."

He smiled at me with genuine affection, and then kissed my hand. "It's very hard for me to say no to you on this, and probably no one else ever will. You're in a unique position to give me a life I can only dream of."

"I know, right?" I took a deep breath and prayed that he would change his mind.

"But Veronica, my life is in Bayou Bend. My academic career has been at Audubon College. It's taken many years to develop my career to this point. Professors don't jump around from university to university. I'll have tenure soon. Besides, Louisiana is my home, I was *born* there. I have two books coming out about Louisiana artists. I'm teaching six classes next semester, my syllabuses are already scheduled for the next two years. I need a woman who can fit into my life." He was gently rubbing my back, trying to reassure me things would be okay.

"You don't need tenure, and I'll publish whatever you want published. I'll make you one of the most successful artists of all time. It just requires clever marketing and lots of money." It is what it is. Claude and I have launched art careers before, more than a few times.

He looked horrified. "Are you really that jaded? Have I taught you nothing over the past four years?"

"Yes, yes, of course you have, but you're an academic," I reminded him, as if he needed it. "You don't live in the art world and don't really know how it works."

Richard looked as though a skunk had walked across the room. "Well, well, well. I guess the student is now the teacher, huh, grasshopper? If my paintings will one day be considered important, that will be left to public opinion. It will not because you decided I win your star search competition, and because you pay a bunch of marketing people to get the world to agree! I don't wish to assume a completely new life. I'm not like you that way," he informed me with an edge of sadness in his voice.

"What is it really, Richard? Is this about something else?"

"That is it *really*," he answered calmly, as if asking me to pass him the butter during a brunch somewhere. "Our paths aren't converging any more. Apparently we're not meant to be. Relationships are difficult enough without forcing outcomes with a thousand pounds of pressure. I believe in fate and listening to the direction of the universe."

"But I love you. I want to be with you forever," I implored him.

"You're not ready," Richard shook his head. "You've played the boyfriend game one time and landed on Braden Davis. That's like being taught how to drive by Dale Earnhardt. And you probably don't really love me, either. Not really. You just see me as a father figure and a teacher. I care about you very much, but it doesn't make sense for me to walk away from everything I've ever known, and assume your life with you on the spur of the moment. My ego would never allow me to be a kept man or whatever. I would resent you for making me give up my life. If you stayed in Bayou Bend, you'd be leaving behind the Musée Fait. Its care requires—and deserves—a constant steward. You have to be that steward." He sighed again, weary from our exchange.

"You just don't want me. That's what this is really about, isn't it?" I noticed the tears welling up but tried to hold them back.

"Yeah, well, maybe it seems that way. But the truth is, I do care about you. I can see myself with you long term. But relationships have to evolve gradually. Long distance relationships don't work; eventually one person has to move to be with the other. Our paths are clear. The universe has spoken."

"Screw the universe!" I yelled dramatically before bursting into tears. "Please think this through. I can give you *anything you want*. If you want a Picasso, you can have it. I can get you three of them, maybe more. Do you want a branch office for Audubon College in Paris? It's yours."

"I don't think so. You've come a long way, but you're still kind of a shit head. You'd hold me hostage in a gilded cage and remind me about it when it suited you. I know you. Forget it. I would end up hating you. Being totally free is central to my worldview, just as it is to yours. At least in that way, we're alike."

"Adjust your worldview! Please! I'll do anything you want; just tell me what would make you happy. I'll set up a trust so you always feel in control and self-sufficient. I'd make it worth your while in every way imaginable. Just tell me what you want. Like how about your parents? They're old and healthcare is expensive. You could give them the best care in the entire world. We'll get them a penthouse at the Mayo Clinic," I pleaded.

"I seriously doubt they have penthouses at the Mayo Clinic," He muttered.

"Whatever! Don't you see?"

He shrugged, and it was clear this conversation was not going to go on much longer. "Yeah, I see. Just not liking what I see."

"One hundred thousand dollars a year. That's what I'll pay you for starters." This was really going down a bad path but I couldn't seem to stop. I had to convince him. I had to have him. "That's probably double your salary."

"What is this, temptation on the mount? Forget it, Veronica." His conviction was pretty hot, if you want to know the truth.

"Two hundred thousand?" I upped the ante, much to his chagrin.

"Wow. I can't believe there's a beautiful genie in front of me begging to grant my wishes, and I want to throw up," snapped Richard, a scowl darkening his handsome face.

I started unbuttoning my blouse. "Stop it, Veronica."

"Three hundred thousand." I got down on my knees and started moving closer to him, hoping to conjure up visions of Mata Hari.

"Cut it out!"

"Four hundred thousand." I was desperate.

"You're really pissing me off. Stop it or . . . "

"Or what? Five hundred thousand. I'm not going to stop. This is not going to stop."

"No!" He roared. "This stops right now! You can't buy me! I don't care how much money you think you have. I'm not for sale. Final! And you've just extinguished any chance of us ever being together. I'm not leaving the college. I live in Louisiana. I'm part of the community—that's who I am and that's where I want to be. You cannot bend me to your will!" He was adamant, and his voice thundered with finality.

He calmed down as I continued sobbing. He sat down and stroked my hair very gently, like he had during the house-sitting incident. "You don't understand anything about love yet because you still don't have the heart of a woman. You're emotionally still a child. But running a multi-million dollar organization should help you mature pretty quickly, one would think."

I corrected him with contempt I didn't feel. "It's now up to a *billion*."

"What a princess you are. Sorry, your highness. But don't you see? You have to follow your own path, as do I. Our paths have converged for years, and now they're separating." His sincerity and resignation was terrifying.

"But I want to be with you, Richard. I want to be with you so much, it hurts."

"I'd love to be with you too, honey. Let's not confuse things. We must obey the universe on this one and not shake our fists at it. That's just the way it is."

"But I'm so scared! I can't do this alone!"

"Of course you can," he said reassuringly. "This is your birthright and your destiny."

"Six hundred thousand! And a memorial library in your name for any city you choose!" I cried.

"It's not an auction. That's it. I'm leaving." He stormed off to get his things, and then headed to the car with me behind him. "You're going to be okay, Mary Veronica," he was telling me. "You can do this. I promise. You need to just stop being a princess and start being a queen."

"What's the difference?" I asked politely, because it seemed like the southern thing to do, but it was pretty hard to focus with a broken heart.

Richard nodded as scores of historical examples raced through his mind. "Well, there are lots of differences. But in general, queens work a lot harder and have much more responsibility. Queens get a lot more respect because of those things. It's not going to be easy, but you'll be okay. You're up for the task."

We stopped at the car. The chauffeur asked me what he should do. I paused, and Richard waited for my response. He wanted to be set free. He wasn't going to be a part of this. He'd seen me at my best and at my worst. He knew I could do anything for him, yet it wasn't enough for him to relinquish his self-reliance. At that moment, as he wielded his character about like Excalibur, I had never loved him more.

"Take him back to Louisiana. Take him wherever he wants to go," I said. It was the hardest sentence I had ever uttered, but keeping him against his will was not an option. I want him to be free, of course. It would just be a lot cooler if his idea of being free was being with me.

Before getting in the car, he pulled me into a big hug that squeezed my tears out even more. "I do care about you, V. I really do. But it's going to have to be from afar." He bent over and gave me the deepest, most romantic kiss you'd ever see in any movie. It almost ripped my soul in half. What a sadist. It certainly was a dirty trick to let me know what I'd be missing on his way out. He rode off into the proverbial sunset, and I immediately aged twenty years.

It then occurred to me that I had been behaving like Claude. That realization was terribly disturbing. The car drove off, and I watched until it disappeared out of sight. The jet would take him home to Louisiana, with my heart in his back pocket. I sat on the front steps of the family empire, now all mine, and cried with my head in my hands. I was all alone with my millions. It wasn't as comforting as you'd imagine. It's nice to have nice stuff, but it's better to have less and someone to share it with who actually likes you. I had blown it with the only person who knew how to take care of me on a psychological level. I wouldn't get to have his kids or take care of him when he was old. Well, you know—older.

My chance at happiness is gone. Claude won, after all.

August 1994

I haven't written much lately. Life has been full of board meetings, social engagements and fundraising dinners. Richard was right. It's not as bad as I had imagined. The responsibility was surprisingly comfortable to throw on. It fits like silk pajamas, a second skin. Musée Fait deserves a faithful steward, and it got one. My life suddenly has a noble purpose and all seems right with the world. It's sad that Claude and I never were able to connect until his last hour of life, but life is like that sometimes.

Richard called me a month ago, to see how things were going. He had lots of advice, as usual. Instead of rolling my eyes as I had so many times in the past, I paid rapt attention because every moment was precious. I grabbed a pen and paper to write down as much of it as possible.

He told me to keep reading and taking classes, to challenge my mind because it turns to mush if you don't. He said not to worry about other people, because they find ways to do what they want to do in the world. He said not to be upset for people who complain constantly about their lives but never do anything to change their stations in life. He said to leave people alone and accept them the way they were and not to judge or control them. He said to focus on the things that truly made me happy.

That was something that took a bit of reflection. Then it hit me. Next door to Musée Fait, I'd create my own café, like Gumbeaux. A place where people could hang out, draw, talk and read for hours. A café complete with art supplies. Easels with drawing paper, paint, charcoal pencils, whatever. An open courtyard to the sky, New Orleans style. A place where creative people will flock for soul warming cuisine, camaraderie and community. I've already asked Dante to look into what kind of permits we will need, and to see if we can use the name "Café Fait." I'll need some more space, though. The people occupying the house next door aren't interested in selling it to me yet, but it's only a question of time. Everyone has their price. Well—almost everyone.

A courier picked up my stuff from Bayou Bend, with some help from George, Betty and Clarence. I actually offered Clarence a job working for me and he's moving here next week.
My life is here in D.C., so I might as well embrace it and stop running away. I'll create a foundation named after my parents to help budding artists and provide scholarships for them. It's time to give back. It's time to share the beauty of the art my parents enjoyed with people from all over the world. I'll create my own art while sharing the art of the great masters. This will ornament people's lives. It will decorate their plates, like the parsley of Willie's comparison. I'll be the parsley on the plates of people's lives, I'll bring color to them—blended color. And that, my friend, is a noble pursuit. At least, it is to me.

7 JE REVIENS

October 2004

I've done philanthropy work all over the world through my foundation. I do all of this anonymously, although I often get found out. It's hard to be mysterious now that we all have internet access. Besides, stewardship isn't about any one person. It's about leaving the things that you've touched with your sphere of influence a little bit better. Just a little bit better.

October 2008

I have been kind of seeing a psychologist. Clarence wouldn't shut up about it so I acquiesced. I wasn't interested in telling her my whole life story so I just handed over my diaries for her to read. She read them and definitely had some hot sports opinions, such as they were.

She said Louisiana was the void in my soul. I haven't been back and avoiding it has only made it bigger in my subconscious. She said the past has kept me from being present in life, and that it feels normal for me to care about people from afar, since I pined away for my parents for all those years (and still do). She said I projected the feelings I had for them onto an actual place. She went on to say that I had been alone so long that I didn't understand how to love anyone, except from a distance. She said to stop longing and start living. As you can see it was a waste of time. What a bunch of pop psychology crap. Right?

I came home with my box of journals and considered putting the whole box in the fireplace. But instead, I took the box and carried it up to the attic, filing it away amongst Christmas decorations and stored summer swimwear. I know it makes me a stronger person to have it around and not to go to it.

June 2009

I'm still seeing the aforementioned psychologist. She talked me into going to Louisiana. Life is ironic. Who would have guessed? I have my own Caribbean island but still daydream about Bayou Bend and Lake Beatrice. Really, it is just the strangest thing, the most unexpected thing. I wish all people could experience great wealth in their lifetimes, just so they could see that it isn't the answer.

I looked up my old friend George Graves on Facebook. He was really happy to get my call; it was just like we'd never been out of touch for a moment. We made plans to stay together at a charming bed and breakfast place we had always admired.

"Is Gumbeaux still there?" I wanted to know.

"No. No, it isn't. Catherine and Willie made a ton of money, got married and moved to Oakland, California. They own a restaurant out there called Muffaletta's. The old Gumbeaux building is a pizza place now." George was still the undisputed gossip king of Bayou Bend.

"Shame."

"Yeah. Shame is right."

"Catherine and Willie got *married?*"

"Yeah. The heart wants what it wants, I guess."

I took the jet down to Bayou Bend. It was great being back. Everything looked exactly the same, except that Gumbeaux was gone. It was comforting in this accelerated culture that there are a few constants. Time moves slower here, there's more reverence for history. George has a life partner named Gerald, a business analyst. In typical George fashion, he told Gerald he was on his own for the weekend because he was going partying with his college sweetheart. Like Louisiana, George hasn't changed much.

We went to the bed and breakfast and checked in. I was pretty revved up to go sightseeing around town. George drove me in his new Range Rover, an anniversary present from Gerald. George had found someone to dote on him, which was exactly what he had always wanted.

First we drove around Bayou Bend. It was impossible to stop smiling. Seeing the sign for Bayou Bend always makes me smile. No matter where I live in my lifetime, no matter how many years and miles away, Bayou Bend will always be my hometown. I lived so much, learned so much, lost so much and loved so much in this magical place. We had so many memories here. Any hesitation about returning melted as the snow.

Then, we headed to New Orleans. We could see riverboat casinos docked proudly at the banks of the Mississippi River. The Georgia pines smelled amazing. Every city has its own particular smell, and this area to me is a combination of pine trees, cayenne pepper and magnolia blossoms. Flowers were bursting everywhere you looked.

We went to all the familiar places, just so I could verify they were still there: Pat O'Brien's, Big Daddy's, Tropical Isle, Cat's Meow, Court of Two Sisters, Preservation Hall, Mulate's, ACME Oyster House, Marie Laveau's Voodoo Museum, the Garden District, Tulane and Loyola, Louis Armstrong Park, Uptown, Jackson Square, the French Market. At Café du Monde, he caught me up on the local gossip for a while. I asked him how Richard was getting along.

George looked surprised. "How is he? Don't you read the alumni magazine? Dr. Landry moved to France, Veronica. He and his family relocated there about four months ago. He's running an extension of Audubon College from Paris now." George grinned and checked out his reflection the rear view mirror. "I've read that all good Americans go to Paris when they die, so Dick must have been super extra good to go there while he was still alive, don't you think?"

Being in Bayou Bend without Richard Landry felt terribly, irrecoverably wrong. It was kind of like Christmas without Jesus. Louisiana without him doesn't seem real because he was the one who introduced it to me. George asked, "You look sick all of a sudden. What's the matter with you?"

"I was hoping to get my soul back," I sighed.

"Uh, okay," responded George dubiously.

"I lost part of my soul here. I came back to find it. I was hoping Richard Landry could help me with that, and now he's gone." I felt really nauseous.

"How can you even remember him? I can't remember what happened two hours ago." George was smoking a Marlborough Light in a cigarette holder, resembling one of the illustrations from

Fear and Loathing in Las Vegas. "Remind me why you stopped seeing Dick in the first place?" George asked. "You never told me the whole story."

"Oh, you know how he was. 'Our paths stopped converging.'"

"Hmmmmmm. Sounds like something he'd say." George looked at me sideways. He seemed to be looking right through me. "Well, anyway, the right guy for you is just around the next bend. Mark my words. And as far as retrieving part of your soul, I'd say you've come to the right place to do it."

"How so?" I asked.

"You know," he insisted.

"Sorry, George, but I don't."

"Come on, Veronica, Voodoo. Right? It's worth a shot."

My eyes got big. "Voodoo? No! No! I have a healthy respect for voodoo and am not screwing around with it. No, no, no!"

"Come on, don't be such a baby," he laughed, encouraging me to get back in the car. "Where's your sense of adventure?"

"But I'm a normal person, George. Normal people don't engage in dalliances with voodoo. I believe in God and Jesus and everything."

George was totally offended. "Oh, and I don't? I'm still a Southern Baptist, Veronica, whether they want me in the club or not. I'm just saying if you want to get something back from the past or from the dead, there's a place to do that."

So, we drove to Hall of Voodoo, and what do you know—Priestess Marie Therese was still there. We went in. She of course knew George and actually remembered me a little bit. "You think there be a curse on you. But that's only if you let it. Don't believe it. The focus of the voodoo experience is to have power over the victim. It is the power of suggestion over the victim's mind. It only works if you *let* it. You have to give your consent."

She went on to tell us that a curse in reality has no power at all. Neither does calling someone bad names. It's the power of suggestion over the psychologically weaker person. Of course it's unpleasant to be informed you're weak minded, but wanting to get better can make you open to anything. She gave me some red powder and said to sprinkle it in my doorways. It seemed pretty silly, and I didn't plan on doing it.

George and I stayed together in the bed and breakfast. We slept in one bed, like we always had during sleepovers at his parents' farm. We giggled and told each other stories and laughed. Being with him again was just lovely. The idea of escaping the long D.C. winters was very appealing. Maybe I could fly south every October with the rest of the snowbirds and then emerge in D.C. each spring like the cherry blossoms. I asked George if he knew any local real estate professionals. He said yes, he did know of one I might like, actually.

George was in the bathroom for a while, and then came out to say he had another curse removal method for me. He said sage was used to lift negative energy, which could cause holes in one's soul. He prepared a bath for me with sea salt and rosemary, and then tied a bunch of dried sage with some string. He lit the end and then blew it out. White smoke emanated from the sage. He waved it around and said to imagine the light of God bathing me in protection. I told him he wasn't qualified to hold voodoo ceremonies, that he didn't know what he was doing, and to stop it immediately. He ignored that and said to repeat three times, "I am cleansed and protected by God's Holy Light." I was then to breathe deeply and know the curse was lifted, and my soul would be whole again. I didn't take much stock in it, but George has a way of getting people to do things.

I woke up to find George had sprinkled red dust all over the floors. He said we should respect all forms of God, not just the Judeo-Christian one from Western Civilization. I told him I was calling the Southern Baptist police to see if I could have his license revoked. He had made a real mess, and I said if he thought I was going to help clean it up, he could punt. He said he didn't know what that meant and sent me off to meet the realtor.

We were meeting at the first of three homes I would see that afternoon. I arrived at a waterfront home on Lake Beatrice, quickly realizing it was one I had admired many times. I parked, tried to get the rest of the red powder off my shoes and walked around the property. There was a boat dock and a small cabin cruiser tied to it. The boat dock had a pergola and was covered in sweet peas. They were flowering beautifully. It looked like an enchanted French country chateau. All at once I felt peaceful and content. There were only the sounds of frogs. Their gentle croaking provided white noise and I imagined the lullaby often lured listeners to sleep.

All of a sudden, the frogs stopped croaking. I looked up to see what had given them pause. The realtor was walking towards me. I started walking to him also. When we got close enough to see each other, we both stopped in our tracks. The realtor was Braden Davis.

Something happened when Braden walked back into my life. It was as though a sledgehammer hit me in the forehead and tweeting birdies were flying directly overhead, as in cartoons. Braden approached me cautiously, as if I might be packing heat, derringer or no derringer.

"Veronica? Is that really you? Really?" That was all he could say.

"Braden? George didn't tell me you were the realtor." He was still a knockout, and I was taken aback. It was kind of funny. He had a *clipboard*. Braden Davis had grown up and he had a normal job. He could barely hold onto his bar jobs as a bouncer when I had known him.

"Yeah, he didn't tell me either. I'm going to have to beat the crap out of him later on this afternoon. You're still so beautiful, it's incredible. Wow. What are you doing these days?" His eyes were like liquid sapphires.

"I work at our family business in Washington. We run a small, private museum." No reason to get into all that now. He looked amazing. Better than ever, really. His hair was just as sexy as ever. No gray in it yet. Soft and black and wavy. His face was still cherubic; eyes still the color of the sea after a storm, mouth sensual. Stanley's mouth.

"Well, if you're going to be a dealer, best to deal in something legal, I always say," he said brightly, tongue firmly in cheek.

"Oh? Since when do you say that?" I tried not to laugh.

"Since I realized that I was driving away everyone I cared about." He stood looking at me intently. "Are you married?"

"No, Braden. I never did that." Something was happening. Something was brewing. The suspense was exhilarating.

"Yeah. I didn't do that either."

"Really? Why not?"

"Oh, you know. Never felt the thunderbolt."

"Yeah, I know what you mean," I said. "It's really nice to see you again. It's nice to meet this version of you. I like it. You're still the star you always were, but you seem a lot less edgy."

Braden shrugged heavily, like he had been beat up by life to the point of surrender. "You want to know the trouble with being a star? Stars have sharp points and deep recesses. They have edges and stick into people. They are unique and cause friction. Stars get in trouble for not looking like the other shapes and not conforming to the rules of geometry, the rules of structure and order. The world punishes the stars and knocks off those sharp points that made them stars in the first place. Suddenly, all we are left with are circles. And the funniest part of all is, then everyone wonders what happened to the stars, and why they are so hard to find. You can't be a star without someone believing in you. I don't think anyone believed in me." He closed his eyes. "That's my philosophy, anyway."

"I always believed in you," I told him sincerely.

Braden hugged me, and his scent was so familiar and appealing. Warmth surged into places long forgotten. It was like standing near a furnace. Then he held me by both shoulders and grinned, locking eyes with me, verifying that the chemistry was mutual. I don't know what my face looked like but clearly it concurred. His expression let me know he might be a little more civilized these days, but he hadn't changed that much- not really. He was still the Braden Davis who fearlessly did whatever he wanted. I had always loved that about him.

"It's still there. I can't believe it's still there," he whispered. All I could do was nod. There's no arguing with a guy like that, even if I hadn't wanted him. Without another word, he picked me up and stormed into the house, making a beeline for the master bedroom. He threw me down on a huge sleigh bed. I wanted to know whose bed it was, and he said something about semantics that didn't make any sense. We went at it for at least an hour, and then collapsed against the white sheets. He held me close and stroked my hair as I shook. It had been a really long time since I had let anyone touch me in that way and had it been anyone else, I would have been terrified. He had become much more attentive, and it was wonderful being with him, even better than before. Then something happened. I noticed that there no longer seemed to be a hole or even a fracture in my soul.

The constant rawness had somehow healed over and was no longer an open wound. I realized at that moment Braden had the missing piece of my soul all this time.

It didn't make any sense. He was the one I would never be able to have. He was a pipe dream. How could I have handed over the shards of my soul to such as unlikely steward? It had to be by far the most reckless of all the poor judgment calls made in my youth. I might as well have tied the Fait fortune to a lottery ticket.

"What happened in California?" I inquired. "Did you get very far?"

He shook his head in a bittersweet sort of way. "No. Not even close. I ended up on the cutting room floor every time. Life is tough in Los Angeles, when you're on the outside. There's a reason they call it 'the jungle.' You have to want it really bad, and you have to know what you're doing. I certainly didn't know what I was doing. You find yourself doing things you never thought you would do. I thought I was a tough guy, but not so much, not out there. At the end of the day and all things being equal, I just wasn't a star after all." He propped up his head with his arm, and used his other hand to play with my hair. It wrenched my heart to hear him say he wasn't a star, and his countenance appeared as though the words hurt him as well.

"You just didn't have a good agent and enough financial backing," I told him softly. It's not over, not if I can help it. He has some stardust left.

He laughed and absently fondled the hem of the Egyptian cotton sheets, trimmed with pale blue satin. "I didn't have any connections whatsoever. My agent turned out to be a total weirdo and kept hinting at the fact that if I was willing to exchange some favors of a sexual nature, things might go my way. I couldn't go through with it. It's never anyone hot, you know. It wasn't even really about that, it was because the other actors were legitimately more talented and had better pedigrees. A guy from acting class actually called me a swamp rat. I beat him up, of course, but it still bothered me. I had to work on my accent and go to elocution lessons. I might have been the best actor in Bayou Bend, but it didn't matter in Hollywood. All the other best actors of their hometowns are there, too.

"Satchmo did a lot better in Hollywood than I did. Every time a director got a glimpse of those titanium fangs, they were scrambling to create a role for him in whatever they were filming at the time. It was a very humbling experience. He was on several television shows and made it into a couple of movies. He even has his own IMDB account, if you can believe it. I would usually just hang out at Paramount or Universal Studios waiting for him all day. People treated me like I was his secretary, and I guess that's all I really was. Then, they found this badass dog handler who Satchmo actually took direction from, and they didn't need me anymore. At that point I was literally just his chauffeur; they didn't even really want me on the lot. We almost got really lucky. HBO was filming a series about Greek Mythology and they wanted Satchmo to pay Cerberus, the three-headed demon dog that guarded the ancient underworld. Unfortunately, Satchmo ended up biting a pretty famous director, who I am unable to name because of a binding legal contract. We both got blackballed from all the major studios after that. It sounds weird but it's fairly standard practice.

"One day I was trying to get Satchmo to go to the beach, since his favorite thing to do was to chase after the waves and try to bite them. He wouldn't get out of bed. I took him to the vet and he was diagnosed with liver cancer. He only lived about two weeks after that. I was absolutely inconsolable and about losing my only friend and decided to give up acting altogether.

"I wasn't ready to leave California, though. I moved to San Diego and became a surfing instructor. That introduced me to a very different world and lifestyle, and it was one adventure after another. My father got very sick five years ago, and I moved home. Since there's nowhere to surf here, I figured I might as well get a real estate license." He sighed, a little spent from both the activity and the monologue. "That's the abridged version of a very long story. Someday, if you're interested, I can tell you the rest."

I assured him that I wanted to hear every last one of his stories, and he possessively hugged me for a long time, and I felt like a commodity. We wrapped ourselves in a couple of the unused towels in the bathroom. They were hotel white and still had tags on them. We went out to the kitchen and made a couple of cups of tea. Braden said he liked to keep refreshments around for his real estate clients, to make them feel more comfortable. Since when had he ever cared about that? Since now, I suppose.

We took our cups of tea to the screened in lanai and watched boats out on Lake Beatrice. A water skier went by. It reminded me that I still needed to call Betty and see how she was making out.

Braden had picked up a pen and slid it behind his ear. He had his clipboard all ready to go. He would have looked much more professional had he been wearing clothes instead of a towel. "So, look, lady, I don't have all day," he sighed in mock impatience. "Are you going to buy the house or not? I mean, what else could I possibly do to persuade you?"

"Not a thing. I love this house and everything about it. I'll take it," I smiled, hugging his arm.

"It's yours, then. And if you really like everything about it, we can come to some sort of arrangement. Maybe I'll end up buying this house for you. Worst realtor ever, but it's so good to see you. I didn't know what the connection was between us then, but it was—and still is—*strong*. The people who really blow your hair back only show up a few times throughout a lifetime. These are the people you never want to lose contact with. To never let go of. They aren't a dime a dozen. The people in your family, the people who loved you when you weren't worth loving, those are the people you keep next to you. Of course you couldn't have stuck around, the way I was going. And I was all about going to California and playing my hand out there. And as you know, I've been around the block, and around the block, and around the block. So, I can tell you for a fact that our kind of chemistry is not everywhere. You think when you're young you'll find it plenty of times. But you just don't."

"No, you don't." This burgeoning connection was coming together organically and not with a thousand pounds of pressure; like when I tried to bend Richard to my will. "Braden? Are you busy this weekend?"

"Yes. What are we doing?"

"I'd like to show you something," I said a little hesitantly, wondering how this conversation was going to turn out.

"What?" he asked, a big question mark across his handsome face.

"My life. My life in Washington, D.C. I have a plane at the airport, so we can go any time."

"Sure, I'm in. Your company must be pretty fancy to have its own plane at the airport. Yes, I'll go with you. You know me, Veronica, I'm a gypsy. I'll go anywhere." He grinned, and it was true. He did have a gypsy heart, which had finally opened, and his best qualities shone through. Besides, I couldn't bear to see my favorite star without his sharp edges and deep recesses. He needed my help. It wasn't too late for him to have the life he had dreamed of. He would actually appreciate it, and that would make me happy too.

Braden really was the one, though it took me years and years to figure it out. He would fit beautifully into my life. He wouldn't object to having money, and he would appreciate what it could do for him. We could be ourselves. We would be able to accept each other for who we really were. **If we can't get the right kind of opportunity for him, then we'll just have to hire a screenwriter to create the content specifically for him. Where there's a will, there's a way and the world is going to be our oyster.**

I don't know why God needed me to wait for so long to find happiness. Maybe it's because if I had spent the last years going on adventures with Braden, I would have slacked off on all the philanthropy work. And maybe it's also because my philanthropy work has made the world just a little bit better-just a little bit. Braden has enabled me to recapture my soul, and I just know everything is going to be fine from this point on. It really is the strangest thing. The most unexpected thing. The strangest, most unexpected, most wonderful thing.

ABOUT THE AUTHOR

Kimberly Vargas manages Modern Postcard's
Human Resources department in Carlsbad, California.
Gumbeaux received a gold medal in the
2011 Readers Favorite fiction contest.
Kimberly lives in San Diego County with her husband Michael.
This is her first novel.